Title and Copyright Page
Reina's Ghosts
MMF Threesome and Werewolf Shifter Romance
Novel
Author: Kay David

From the Publisher:
Thank you for purchasing this book.

Table of Contents

Reina's Ghosts
Description

"...We'd always been told stories about the white wolf, but I always thought they were a myth. I mean a were wolf who was not controlled by the full moon? That was too good to be true. Until I became one myself, the first white wolf in over a century..."

Reina's life had been one big failure, until she became the one thing every wolf in the world wanted. She became the most wanted werewolf in the world.

Troy and Darren are the perfect couple, they had the perfect lives and perfect jobs to go with it. It looked like nothing would ever go wrong until one rainy night in Las Vegas, everything changed. On a trip back from a wedding, they came across an injured and unconscious Reina. Troy immediately recognized her as one of his kind. He smelt the wolfsbane on her and knew that she could only mean trouble. She was a threat to every single secret he had tried so hard to hide from his beloved Darren.

He insisted they abandon her or call 911, but Darren would have none of it. They take her back to L.A with them and so begin a chain of events that would change their lives forever and a love that Reina had never thought she would be worthy of receiving despite the ghost of her past.

Prologue

Gloucestershire, England

1st January 2019,

The group of men stood around a very large stone slab which served as a table of some sort. They were twelve in number and wore similar garbs of black cloak, like something off of an old England magic movie. Although given the current situation one could say it was a magic movie minus the old England since the year was 2020.

They were walking in slow circles round the large stone slab and murmuring words only they could understand in unison, it was some form of old Gaelic language spoken by the Celtic people of Wales. They were in a cave close to the Severn river along the border between England and Wales and the cold air was blowing gusts of wind into the cave making the fire lanterns quiver forming various shadows on the cold walls of the cave.

There was blood smeared on each of their foreheads and it was a drawing of an inverted triangle inside a box. They were all holding a werewolf totem which was shaped like a double-edged axe with a handle on its end.

A young woman was lying on the stone slab, she was wearing a white dress and her skin was so pale it was almost as if she was dead except that her chest rose and fell with each breath that she took signifying that she was still alive. Her hair was as black as night it was almost blue and it was a sharp contrast to her pale complexion. Her hands lay useless beside her but she was not bound to anything. There were small pots surrounding where she lay and its content was some reddish black liquid like blood.

The men suddenly stopped and raised their hands. One of them stepped out and picked up one of the pots at the foot of the young woman and walking to her head, he smeared it with the reddish-black liquid drawing the same symbol on his head on hers. Then he stepped back and said a chant

"Onc bina tha tieges sinc onkf"

The whole group repeated this after him over and over again, the girl started shaking violently on the stone and two of the men quickly went and held her down,

"Is this supposed to be happening?" One of the men holding her down asked in bewilderment, looking up at their leader. He had a thick old English accent and it made what he said almost in decipherable. Their leader was the man that had smeared the red liquid on the girl's head.

"Hold her down," he answered and motioned to the other men to continue with the chant. They continued and this time raising their voices louder, the girl began to shake violently and the breeze coming into the cave became more and more fierce causing the fires to move with the wind. But the men did not relent still, they continued chanting faster and louder until the girl made a shrill and screeching sound like that of a banshee.

"She's too strong, I don't if we can hold her for much longer," the other man holding her legs motioned for some more men and they joined in to hold her down. While the others were still saying the chant

The woman stopped screaming and moving suddenly and the fires immediately went out. It was eerily quiet for about 10 seconds before there was a sharp shriek,

"Cedric, is that you? What is it?"

There were no lights and the men were scrambling trying to put lights back on, almost immediately, the lights came back on and the cave was flooded with lights. But something was very wrong, two of the men lay on the floor in their own pool of blood, they had been battered as if by a wild animal and the woman on the slab was nowhere to be seen.

Chapter 1

Los Angeles, California.

Troy Dalton was running, he had no idea what was chasing, he did not even know if he was being chased. All he knew was that something was coming for him and he needed to get to the girl. She was his destiny, the raven-haired girl with the tattoos. He had been seeing her for months now, she was always crying, always calling out to him. But he never caught her, she was always out of reach. And they always took her, he didn't know who they were. But he knew they were dangerous, and leaving her with them was the worst thing he could do.

He had no idea who the girl was, he just knew he had to help her, so he continued running, no matter how futile his efforts always seemed to be.

"Troy! Troy!" the voice calling at him was faint yet it sounded very loud in his head, like it was coming out of the very loudest speakers. The un-realness of it all did not make sense to him.

Where was she? Why do I never see her face? Troy thought to himself.

He only saw her back, her hair as black as a raven's feathers. So long it almost got to her back, and her bare feet which was bloody from all the running she had been doing in the forest.

"Thump! Thump!"

The footsteps of the men coming behind him grew louder, the faster he ran, the louder their sound seemed to grow.

"This way, I saw her go this way," one of the men spoke to the others, directing them to where the girl was running to.

He had a very thick accent, he was not sure which country it was but he thought it was probably Irish or Scottish. He almost could not make out what they were saying because of the thick accent. He shouted as loud as he could so as to distract them from going after the girl, but it was almost like he was invisible. They went after her with so much determination totally ignoring his existence.

Swoosh

The sound of an arrow whizzed past him as he immediately crouched down to avoid getting hit.

Who the hell are these guys? he thought to himself as he got behind a big tree and hid himself with its massive body.

The men continued to advance as they shot more arrows at the girl. She managed to dodge them all and Troy just hid there, unsure of what next to do.

"Troy! Troy!"

Just as he was about to stand up and continue his search for the girl, one of the guys spoke up. "I have her," and then out of the blue, some men grabbed him by the hands and began pulling him farther away from her.

"No! No! Get your filthy hands off of me." He struggled against their tight grip as they took him away, but all his struggles were useless against their strength and the men only ignored him.

"I need to save her! I need to get to her! Get off me!" He continued his struggle.

"Troy! Troy, wake up, you're having a nightmare." Someone shook him, as the familiar voice roused him awake.

"Where is she, I need to get to her..." Troy sat up still talking to himself as he realized he was now awake and he had been having a bad dream. His partner and husband,

Darren, of about 2 years held him, trying to calm him down. He was sweating as if he had just finished running a marathon and breathing very hard.

"You need to get to who, babe? It was just a dream. You're okay now." Darren said still trying to get him to calm down.

"You were talking loudly in your sleep. Do you want to talk about it? Sounded really bad. Was it the same dream?" Troy nodded his answer to Darren disentangling himself from his grasp.

"Yes it, was." He had been having the same recurring dream for over 2 months now and he had no idea why. He kept seeing the same girl over and over again, she was always running and the same group of men were always hunting her, but he was never able to save her neither was he ever able to get the guys, they always got him. He never saw the girls face but he felt like he had known her for ages.

Darren had been disturbing him, trying to get him to talk about the dream or even see a shrink, but he could not do that, he doubted anyone would understand. And he was not in the habit of paying some stranger an abominable amount of money to talk about his 'feelings'. He had a feeling the girl from his dream was of his 'kind', and even though he had been with Darren for over 3 years now, two of which they had been married, he had not been able to tell him about his true identity, he knew there was no way he could tell him now, it would probably scare him away, and he was not going to take any chances on the instance that the love of his life may or may not leave him.

"I still think you should see Dr. Pevesh. She's like the best Psychologist in LA. I even heard that Ben Affleck used her the last time he fell off the wagon. And you obviously have some issues you need to let out since you can't talk to me about them."

Troy rolled his eyes at the mention of Ben Affleck. Darren was almost obsessed with Hollywood stars.

"I can't talk about this now, Darren. I need you to please understand. Whenever I am ready, you'll be the first person I talk to and not some shrewd shrink in Harry Potter glasses telling me I have mommy issues."

"She's not a shrew, T. Don't be sexist and besides she has like 8 million followers on Instagram so bite your tongue. But I get it, I will give you space and the time you need, but we have been together for over 3 years now and we are married for two and I need you to be honest with me. I need to know all of you."

"And you will, you already do. This dream or whatever it is doesn't change anything. It's probably just because of what I'm going through at work and it doesn't mean anything."

Darren gave him an 'are you kidding me" look, but he let it slide. He knew he was full of shit but he did not call him out on it, he always tried as much space as he could, and this was one of the reasons Troy loved him. He never smothered him or anything of the sort, instead, they gave one another space and respected each other's privacy while at the same time tried to communicate to one another all the time.

"Try and get some sleep then. You're going to need it in the morning." He kissed him and got back to bed.

Troy however laid down on the bed, but he could no longer fall asleep, his thoughts went back to the dream, he could not get it out of his mind. He had never felt so helpless in his life and he hated that feeling of helplessness more than anything, it brought back memories he would rather not remember.

He had a feeling something was coming, something dreadful and ominous, he had no idea what it was but one thing he knew for sure was that the girl in his dreams, whoever she was, she was not good news and he had a stronger feeling it was just a matter of time now before everything came crashing down. He just hoped at the end of it all, Darren and himself would be fine.

*****

Las Vegas, Nevada.

May 28th 2019

"Reina! You can't run forever now." The sounds of the men shouting her name intensified the faster she ran, the faster they were on her trail.

"Whack! Whack! Whack!

The sounds coming from the bushes around her as she ran. Reina knew she had to keep running. Her legs were killing her. They were torn up, bruised and bloody from running for over one hour barefooted in the woods, but she didn't dare stop, a far worse fate awaited her if she did.

She was wearing a transparent night gown and the cold was biting at her skin, there were scratches on her arms and legs from the sharp edges of the grasses all around her, but even all these did not deter her from her escape, she would rather die and even walk through hell back before she allowed herself to be captured by these men. She knew what they were after, and knew that she would rather die than let them have it. She followed the direction her heart was telling her to.

Two weeks earlier

After her escape from the Twelve, Reina thought she was finally free from Ziro and his men, so she let her guard down with the family that had taken her in. They had offered her safety, a *stranger*. But they had done it with so much love and open-heartedness it felt like she had known the McCullens forever. And to show her gratitude, Reina had begun to work for them at the tiny antique store they owned. They had treated her like the daughter they never had, and sadly they paid dearly for it with their lives.

She had been staying with them for a little over three months after her escape, wandering around England without anything but the clothes on her back before she had been taken in by the McCullens. One cold morning, she had woken up to find the house quiet and empty, thinking nothing of it, since the McCullens were early risers. She got prepared for work and locked up the house before she went on her way to the store. She even bought the blueberry muffins and special tea Mr. McCullen always liked.

Just as she arrived at the entrance of the store, she saw the closed sign, wondering why the doors were still closed since it was already 9 am, she used her own spare key they had given her to open the door calling on Sarah McCullen as she was going in, before she took another step into the store, she was grabbed from behind and her worst fear had just come through, before she could scream his and covered her mouth.

She looked around the store looking for John and Sarah, but they were nowhere to be seen and there was blood on the counter. She began to struggle with her assailant trying to get away and see if she could save the McCullens.

Ziro, the leader of the Twelve, stepped forward while one of his lackeys dragged Sarah in by her hair as she was still trying to plead with them and weeping as she did so, grabbing Sarah from the man who held her, Ziro pulled her to him, her back to his front and held a knife to her throat.

"Ziro, please let her go. You already have me. They're innocent and don't know anything. Please don't hurt them, just take me."

Reina was hysterical now as she pleaded and pleaded for him to let her go but all her pleas fell on deaf ears.

"Oh sweet, sweet Reina, I plan on taking you. But them, I have no use for them, but they will serve as a lesson to you." He smiled menacingly as he toyed with the knife around her neck and Sarah whimpered in fright.

"This is exactly what will be the fate of any individual you decide to run to, so next time you decide to escape and trust me. There will be no next time, you will think again before you ask the help of a poor, helpless human."

"Please! Please don't do this." Ziro simply ignored her pleas as he slashed the knife across Sarah's throat ripping it as blood gushed out and she slumped on the floor and stopped moving.

The men in the room, whom she had not even noticed before now began to cheer as she crumpled down crying and calling Sarah's name even though she knew she was dead. Suddenly they pushed a white hanky over her face, and she lost consciousness. Her last thought before the darkness closed in on her was as she wondered what had happened to Mr. McCullen.

*****

Reina woke up with a start, her vision was blurry as she tried to get used to the harsh sunlight streaming into the place she was lying on the cold floor, her vision was blurry as she tried to get used to the tiny dimly lit room she was in. her throat was very dry and she was so thirsty she could drink a whole river, she looked.

She looked around her surroundings trying to remember what she was doing in such a place and how she got there. Then it all started to come to her slowly, she remembered yesterday morning as she went to the McCullen's store only to get waylaid by Ziro and his men.

They had killed the only people who had truly cared of her. She remembered the look on Sarah McCullen's face before her throat was slit like a lamb offering. That look of hopelessness and disappointment would hunt her for the rest of her life. They hadn't deserved what they got, they had lived simple lives, minding their business and selling their beautiful antiques in their store.

The only crime they had committed was trying to help a stranger and they had paid dearly for it with their lives. She could not even blame Ziro or the Twelve, No, she only had herself to blame for the misfortune that befell John and Sarah.

She had known how dangerous Ziro could be and she had brought danger to their doorstep by living with the McCullens and now they were dead. She could only hope that that they were in a better place and that they were together.

Her next thought was how she was going to survive this and escape fast. She needed an escape plan, but how could she come up with one when she did not even know where she was. Her hands and her feet were bound by very hard rope and given the way they were burning into her skin, she was sure they had been laced with wolfsbane.

The room was dimly lit with only one door, the walls were narrow and long and the only source of ventilation was the tiny window so high that her hands could not even reach it unless she used a ladder. Ziro had definitely thought all this through before he had even recaptured her. That meant they had been so sure they were going to capture her. They had probably watched her for days or even weeks before waiting for the right moment to pounce.

That would explain the feeling of being watched she had been feeling for the past few days. She had been so sure she was safe in the tiny village with John and Sarah.

She tried to struggle against the ropes, but they only burnt her skin harder, she couldn't even use her powers to set herself free thanks to the wolfsbane. Just as she still was trying to figure out her next move, she heard footsteps and then voices just outside the door.

"I need water!" she shouted at the top of her lungs, trying to get them to hear her. There was only silence as whoever was behind the door ignored her, she continued to scream and when it was obvious that no one was going to come to her aid, she pushed herself towards the door, crawling like a snake since her hands and feet were tied up. When she got to the door, she began to bang on it until one of the men in anger opened a small partition on the door which she had noticed earlier and pushed a small cup of water inside.

She was able to get up on her feet and collect the water bringing the liquid to her mouth and satisfying her thirst. The man muttered 'bitch' before he snapped the partition shut. She simply ignored it and bided her time as crawled back to her previous position. She would save her strength until the right opportunity presented itself, and then she would make her escape, and she would kill anyone that stood in her way including the asshole who just called her a bitch.

After about 30 minutes although she could not be sure, there were more sounds of footsteps coming toward the door, and then the sound of rattling keys in the keyhole, before the door was flung open.

Ziro the leader of the Twelve and Head Alpha of Uktena werewolf tribe in England, walked in like the alpha boss that he was, he walked in with two other men and Reina and Reina could not be sure if they were also among the Twelve, Ziro was the only one of them she really knew.

He was wearing a plaid suit, his black hair sleeked back like some mafia boss, He casually strolled in his face lacking any expression whatsoever, she couldn't tell if he was angry or not.

"You are back in the states, Las Vegas to be precise." He stopped waiting to see the effect his words had on her. She showed no emotion whatsoever, calmly waiting for him to complete what he wanted to say. Although her insides were in turmoil, her only thought was her escape, but she was wondering what they were doing in Las Vegas. She thought of all the places she could disappear to in Nevada or even California. Her thoughts were interrupted when Ziro continued.

"I've decided that you're more trouble than you are worth and I'm selling you to the Nevada Wendigo pack."

Oh no, not again. she thought to herself.

"They've been so benevolent that they are not going to kill you yet, they need your blood, as much of it as possible and are even willing to share your power with us, whatever is left of you after that you can keep it."

"Fuck you, Ziro, you are not getting one drop of my blood. I would rather die before I let you do that." She spat on him as she spoke, although given the distance between them, it didn't have the desired effect.

Ziro simply laughed at her outburst, aggravating her even more.

"Oh sweet Reina, believe me, I would kill you myself, if it were up to me, but you are pretty special to whole werewolf clan and I can't do that just yet."

She simply stared at him, allowing her face convey all the hatred she was feeling in her heart, and do all the talking for her.

"I'm off now to meet with my business partners, why don't you be a good girl and sit tight." The way he said "business partners" made it clear he was going to meet with the people he was trading her to.

"In the meantime, enjoy the wolfsbane in your blood, you understand it's for our protection, right? We can't have you going all white werewolf on us mere peasants again and killing someone else." He said the last part with so much venom that she could feel the hatred and jealousy radiating off of him.

Reina could only wonder what he had ever done to him to stir such feelings in him, he had been her mentor at one point and she had always viewed him as the father figure she never had when her own real father failed to be one to her, but she guessed her powers were the only thing he had been after from the very beginning when he had found her and pretended to be on her side.

"I will kill the lot of you the first chance I get," she told his retreating back as he walked out of the room. He stopped for a second and looked back at her, and then he walked out slamming the door and locking it with a sharp click.

****

L.A, California.

13th May, 2019.

It was a full moon tonight, Troy sat on the stool in front of the kitchen counter as Darren was making dinner for the both of them. He was finishing off with a few emails he had brought home from work, trying to listen to the work story Darren was entertaining him with, even though his mind was elsewhere and he only had half his attention on what Darren was saying.

"...so she came back from the O.R after about 3 hours in surgery. The surgeon who had attended to her was literally a first year resident, who was basically a doctor still in diapers, and botched up the whole thing. Her boobs were not the same size, one was the size of a cabbage, the other was the size of an apple, while her ass which she also had a butt lift done, was sagging. The whole thing was hilarious given the seriousness of the situation. She's suing the clinic."

Troy laughed out loud with him as he finished his story, even though he had only listened to half of what he had said. "Wow, that is bad."

"Right? I always say, if you're going to get a plastic surgeon, get a recommendation from the Kardashians, and not some whack clinic cuz you're trying to save money." He laughed at his own joke while stirring the soup he had cooking on the stove.

Troy looked at him with affection. Darren was quirky and chatty all at once. He could talk your mind off anything. It was one of the things he had hated about him when they had first met, ironically. They had met about five years ago at UCLA teaching hospital, when Troy had been involved in an accident and Darren had been the resident doctor attending to him.

They had hated each other at first although Darren had been secretly crushing on him. Troy was dating his girlfriend at that time Jessica and he had no idea he was attracted to guys, he had never even imagined himself with another guy until Darren.

Darren had come to check on him almost every day while he had been in the hospital and when they had finally started talking, he had found himself looking forward to Darren's routine check-ins. When he had been discharged, they had remained friends and even went for out for drinks for a while although it was platonic at that time. However their friendship had blossomed into more and now he realized that Darren was the love of his life and there was no one else for him.

After Darren finished his cooking, they had dinner in comfortable silence, only talking about work and some other mundane things. They cleared up the dishes together, even though he wanted to do it alone Darren insisted he would help. They cleared up the dishes and then Darren went up to clean up and to bed while Troy remained downstairs in the living room to finish up some work.

Two hours later, Troy went up to bed and joined Darren. A little after midnight, Troy crept out of bed careful not to wake Darren lest he had to explain his whereabouts to him and skip out on what he had been looking forward to all week. He needed the freedom and perspective his transformation always gave him.

He had been having dreams about a girl whom he had never seen before but she seemed so familiar, he felt like he knew everything about her. His gut told him she was a wolf but he could not even be sure why he was having such feelings trying to forget about his very bizarre dream, he changed into his workout gears even though he was not going to work out, but he wore it so he would have something to tell to Darren if he came back and found him awake.

He hated lying to him but he had no choice, at least for the time being, he had to protect their relationship. It was the most precious thing to him.

Taking his crescent band, he walked quietly out of the house and jogged past the array of houses on their streets to a much quieter part of town and into the woods. When he got to the thicker part of the woods where he was sure no one would come along, he took his clothes off and stood naked under the moonlight, reveling in its radiance, when the moon reached its peak, he felt his bones begin to crack and then fracture as they took on the shape of a were wolf.

The pain which he was already used to from over 13 years of turning racked his body as a spurt of hair growth covered his arms and his entire body, the claws on his fingers and feet also began to extend out of his skin causing another bout of pain. His eyes took on the color of burning embers of fire piercing the night with its brightness as his transformation became complete.

"Awhooooooo."

His loud howl rendered into the cold and quiet woods, echoing loudly and piercing the quietness of the night, he did it one more time before he began to run with the speed of a cheetah. He ran deeper into the woods as the breeze zipped past his ears, he felt all his worries and fears fade away into nothing as he continued to run, he ran until he lost record of time and place. When he was finally exhausted, he sprinted to where he had left his clothes and changed back into his human form before putting on his clothes and jogging back home.

Day had begun to break by the time he got back to the house and finding it quiet and empty, he went into the kitchen to have a glass of water thirsty from all the running. He found a note stuck to the refrigerator, it was in Darren's handwriting.

Got called early into work for an emergency surgery, I took the liberty of making you coffee. Hope you had a good run, have a wonderful day. Love D.

Troy smiled to himself as he read it again. He really was a lucky man.

Chapter 2

After Troy finished with his coffee, he went up to get prepared for work. About an hour and thirty minutes later, he locked up the house, got into his car and drove out of their garage getting to work in record time. It was almost 8:30 by the time he arrived at the office, his assistant, Jane, a tiny Latina in her early forties, met him as he was entering the building shoving a cup of Starbucks in his face.

He collected it from her smiling as she gave him a reproachful look. She was the only one that could give him that look and get away with it, apart from Darren of course. Jane had been his assistant for over 7 years now and they had grown very close over the years that she treated him like her son even though the age gap between them wasn't even that much.

"You're late." They walked into the building together as she spoke.

"Jane, I wonder sometimes who's the boss between the both of us." Troy was laughing at her antics as they got into the elevator together.

"Yeah, yeah, we know you're the boss, but you can't do without me so that makes me kind of a boss in my own right," she said tongue in cheek.

Tony laughed at that. "What do I have today?" he asked.

"The meeting you were supposed to have with the people from ALAEX firm's been delayed by 20 minutes, I emailed you this morning, but I'm guessing you haven't seen it yet."

"No."

"Well, Drew already told them it was going to cost them, surprisingly they agreed without any hassle, said the delay was unavoidable."

"Okay, is Drew in the office right now?" Troy asked as they got out of the elevator. Drew was his partner in the firm.

"Nah, he stepped out a few minutes ago, said it was urgent." Troy simply wondered what was so urgent that he had to leave so early in the morning before the day even began.

"Okay, what about after the meeting, did you reschedule my meeting with the team from San Francisco, I won't be able to make it that week, Darren's brother is getting married then."

"Oh, I already did that, but I had no idea it was because of Darren's brother's going to get hitched, that is great news," she gushed. Jane had always had a soft spot for Darren, she loved him obviously more than her own boss. But who could blame her, Darren could make a serial killer fall in love with him.

"How's Darren anyways? I haven't seen him in a while, he's probably too busy saving lives." They had gotten off the elevator onto their own floor and were now entering his office. Jane trailed behind Troy as he entered his large spacious office. The walls were transparent and it overlooked the LA skyline, the sight was breathtaking.

"He's good, he's been asking about you too. I hope the both of you are not planning behind my back to leave me and get married to each other," Troy joked, settling down on his desk and booting his laptop.

"Oh trust me, when I want to steal your man, you wouldn't even know what hit you." They both laughed.

"We should go on a double date," Troy groaned at her suggestion, already dreading it.

"Yeah me, you, Darren and Harry, let's catch up." Harry was Jane's husband of about 12 years, they had all gotten close over the years Jane had been working for Troy.

"That'd be great Jane, check my schedule and set something up. I'll check with Darren, although I'm sure he's gonna say yes."

"Cool, will that be all, I don't think you have any other appointment set up today, but I'll let you know if anything comes up." She was already walking out when Troy remembered something.

"Oh and Jane, could you order me two sets of cufflinks for the wedding, Darren's been going on about it and I decided to buy them to try and take some of the stress off his shoulders."

"Aww look at you being all domestic and homely, who knew that Darren would be the reason for all these positive changes." Troy simply gave her a pointed look and she immediately got serious.

"Two sets of cufflinks coming right up," she fake saluted him and left the office.

.....

After the meeting ended, Troy was walking back to his office with Drew, all tensed up and looking stressed, they were talking about some of the issues they had discussed in the meeting. The meeting didn't go exactly as planned and they were both livid.

"I'll talk to you later man, I have another meeting with some new clients," Drew said walking away and Troy simply nodded still heading to his office. Jane approached him tentatively, very much aware of the mood he was in.

"You're scheduled for a 2pm conference call with some of the execs from Universal studios, they want you to bring them up to speed on their ad investment."

"Cancel it," he said not stopping to listen to whatever she still had to say as he got into his office and slammed the door.

Not one to back down, Jane entered his office after him and continued.

"You already cancelled this meeting once before, they won't take too kindly to another cancellation, Sir," she always used 'sir' whenever she knew he was pissed off.

"Fine, tell them I'll be available," Troy didn't care whether they were pissed off or not, that was their business but he had to play nice with them since they were one of their biggest clients. He looked up to find Jane still standing there and not saying anything.

"What else?"

"They're already on the line, sir. It's 2pm."

"Fuck! Well put them on the line then."

"Done," she said as she strutted out of the office, leaving him to take the conference call.

Standing up and facing his large window, looking out at the view, Troy put the call on speaker as he listened to the stuffy execs from Universal Studios as they talked about how well they expected the ad for their new feature film to do.

"I oversaw the campaign personally Mr. Shapiro, the billboards are already up, and YouTube already advertises the ad on every new music video that comes out for the next week." Troy pointed out for the hundredth time.

"If you want to have more exposure given to the film, you need to stall the money and let me do the job you're paying my firm to do."

"That is not an option, Mr. Dalton. The premier date is already fixed," he replied adamantly.

"Then you have to let me work with the time and material I currently have at my disposal."

There was silence for a few minutes, as they considered what he said, before somebody else, this time a woman told him.

"Well, given the fact that this is going to be a feature film, we can extend its premiere for a couple of weeks, two at the most, to give you time to fix it."

Troy heaved a sigh of relief not even having the energy to reply the jab she made at him "fixing it." There was no amount of advertising that could boost the sales of the film, and they knew it. It was some indie chick flick that wouldn't have seen the light of day save for the fact that Brad Pitt was in it. It was his firm that had raised its points a little.

"That will be better, I will have my assistant mail you a few of the results. Are we done here?"

"I hope the results turn out great, Dalton."

"They will." He clicked off not giving them any opportunity to say something else. Bunch of stuff assholes. He thought to himself as he got back to his desk and tried to focus on the work he still had to do, suddenly there was a knock on his door.

"Come in," he called out in curiosity since he was not expecting anyone.

A face peeked in around the door before scrambling into his office, "Hey, Mr. Dalton," Beck, one of the firm's IT guys said as he walked closer to Troy's desk.

"Hey," Troy indicates towards his chair and he promptly sits, Beck was a fresh MIT graduate, who got employed as soon as he had graduated summa cum laude from his class, his IQ charts were off the roof and he was a nerd to the bone, complete with the Harry Potter glasses. Even his fashion sense screamed 'geek alert'.

"What can I do for you Beck?" Troy asked although he already suspected his reason for stopping by his office. His department was in charge of monitoring the progress of the online ads, they had for a bunch of clients.

"Well," he coughs and sits back as he tried to maintain eye contact making it painfully obvious that he was nervous. Troy had a reputation for being hardass to some of the staff.

"Some of the ads we have YouTube aren't doing so well, the numbers are really low and only going down by the minute."

"So..." Troy prompts, hoping he didn't come to him with a problem without a viable solution. He didn't mind problems, so long as he was given a proposed solution to said problem.

"So, I had a meeting with some of our media specialist and the social media director," he goes on making Troy smile on the inside, proud that he wasn't going to be disappointed.

"They're interviewing people right now, trying to get more people to help with marketing the film ad and increasing its probability to skyrocket in sales."

"Is the time and cost doable?" Troy asked trying not to show how impressed he was, he guessed his MIT certificate was not a waste.

"They're all under budget, sir."

"Good," he said simply returning to his computer and continuing his work. The door to his office opens and he glanced up to see Beck's retreating back, his walk having a little swagger in it and his head lifted in pride.

Troy loved initiative. The senior staff in the firm always pushed the junior ones to be better in everything by giving them work that enabled them to show what they were capable of and from the looks of it they were never disappointed.

******

Darren stood in front of his patient who was 19 year old young girl as she was flanked by her parents on both sides as they all tried to look strong. She had been diagnosed with Lupus over 2 years ago and now her kidney was failing so she needed a kidney transplant. Darren was giving them their options.

"Like I said before Tory, the lupus has caused an inflammation of some blood vessels that filters wastes in your kidney by attacking them, so this has caused your kidney to stop doing its function," he stopped for a while allowing that information to sink in before he continued.

"It's a condition called End Stage Renal Disease (ESRS), and at this point you're going to need a kidney transplant--"

"I volunteer! You can take my kidney for the transplant," her mother added quickly not even allowing Darren to complete his sentence as she tried to save her daughter's life by any means necessary.

"That's very commending, Mrs. Hastings, because the waiting list is going to be a very long one. But there are a lot of things we need to take into account before considering you as a possible option for the transplant. One of them being to confirm if you are going to be a match." Darren explained gently as he tried to sound both professional and sympathetic all at once. This was one part of his job he actually hated. Having to tell the family the hard truths.

"Well what is there to confirm. I'm her mother, I'm sure we're going to be a match," she replied, unwaveringly.

"If my wife' not a match then you can use mine," her father chipped in trying to be a pillar of support for his family as he held his wife's hand who in turn takes Tory's hand into hers and squeezing it.

"Of course, but before we consider either of you, we will have to first run a series of tests to ensure that both your blood work and tissues are a match. Also, we have to evaluate Tory herself if she is going to be indeed strong enough to undergo such a major surgery. Since you're still so young then there's a high chance that she will be. But until then, we are going to place you under a dialysis treatment for now, until everything is in place and we can schedule a date for the surgery."

"Of course, Dr. Darren, money is no issue, we want the best treatment for Tory, she's our only daughter," Mr. Hastings pleaded, albeit sounding a bit conceited but who could blame him, his only daughter was about to undergo a life changing surgery.

Nodding his head, Darren faced Tory speaking pointedly to her.

"I hope you're going to be ready for a strict lifelong medication regimen after the surgery, Troy," she simply nodded her head in reply as she held unto her mother trying to be strong and not fall apart in front him.

After giving them the full analysis, Darren gave them some privacy to talk about what they intended to do going forward.

"Darren loved his job, he loved being a doctor. He also loved the fact that he had the ability to change the course of a patient's life for the better, but one of the things he hated most besides losing a patient was, having to deliver bad news to the family of the patient. He dreaded such moments with so much passion, but he knew they were unavoidable, one had to take the bad with the good. It was one of the quirks of being a health worker. You win some, you lose some, but the winning made up for the losses one hundred percent. It made everything they did worth it.

As he walked out of the hospital building to the café for his break, some of his co-workers and friends were already seated there nursing different cups of coffee in their hands and comparing notes about one or two procedures they had done that day.

Darren joined them, taking the last available seat on their table just as one of the waitresses approached him and took his order.

"Rough day?" Paul, one of the doctors asked him as he heaved on the chair.

"You don't even know the half of it, I just had to tell a family of three that one of them may or may not survive a kidney transplant," he drank from his coffee which had just been placed in front of him as he spoke.

"That's rough man," someone else commented.

"I just told a mum that her 3 year old son's just been diagnosed with lymphoblastic leukemia," Paige said as she stared hard at her cup of coffee as if trying to fight back the tears that was brewing in her eyes.

"It was all I could do not to bawl my eyes out right there, my daughter's five and I cannot even imagine going through that."

They all kept quiet for a while, trying to collect their thoughts and emotions.

"Well that went downhill pretty fast," Diego said, trying to cheer them up, and some of them even smiled.

"On a brighter note, I helped deliver a set of twins today through a c-section, mom and babies are all in one piece," they all laughed at that, giving Diego a grateful look for breaking the bad tension.

He simply shrugged his shoulders and smiled with them.

"On an even brighter note," Darren said. "My baby brother's getting married in two weeks." He beamed using his hands to blow a fake trumpet in mock jubilation. They all laughed with him.

"If I had a dollar for every time you made that announcement, Darren, I would be a very rich woman," Paige said to him rolling her eyes playfully.

"Who even gets this excited over going to a family wedding," Paul asked on exasperated tone.

"Well obviously Darren does," this came from Diego.

"You guys can laugh all you want but what can I say, it's not a crime to love my brother so much that I am so happy he has finally found marital bliss."

"Marital bliss who even talks like that, Darren?"

They all laughed at that. And not after a few more jabs, they stand up to go and resume their shift some of them promising to send gifts to the soon to be married couple since they would not be able to attend the wedding.

. . .

That evening, both Darren and Troy sat in their living room in comfortable silence as they both work on their laptops. They had just finished having dinner of cold pizza and were winding down before they went to bed.

31

"Hey babe, Jane asked about you today," Troy said making Darren wake up from what he was doing.

"Aww how's she doing, I haven't seen her in a while."

"She said the same thing. She wants us to have dinner, the four of us including Harry."

"Yeah, that'd be cool. I was actually thinking we should have date night this weekend, just the two of us. But it'll be nice for Jane and Harry to join us, we can catch up on all the gossip," he said the last part with a wink and Troy only smiled at that.

"I wouldn't expect anything less. I'll tell her to set it up."

"I'm beat, it was a tough day at work today. I think I'll head up to bed."

"What happened at work?" Troy asked him, a look of concern flashing across his face.

"I had to inform two parents that their only daughter was going to need a kidney transplant very soon or she might die."

"Shit, that's gotta be rough, I don't even know how you do it."

"It was rough, but there's a silver lining I guess. The parents are both offering to donate their kidney, so whichever of them is a match, the surgery can be done as soon as we've carried out all the necessary tests."

"That's good news right?"

"Yeah it is," he smiled at him, giving him a lingering kiss on the lips.

"At least I have my brother's wedding to look forward to." He beamed as he mentioned Zack's upcoming wedding

"Well, there's that." Troy smiled with him, amused at how the mention of his brother's wedding could lift his mood so quickly.

"I had Jane order the cufflinks you'd been stressing over today," Troy notified him.

"Oh my God! I love you, you are a life saver!" Darren said, kissing him again on the lips and his jaw.

"I'm only happy to be of help babe, I hate to see you all stressed out, please tell me if there's anything more I can do." Troy held his hand as he spoke earnestly to him.

"Oh I will, but you've done more than enough by just being you," he replied affectionately even though he knew how cheesy he sounded.

"Are you coming up with me?"

"Oh, I will be up shortly, I just need to finish off a few last minute details on this new ad campaign I'm working on."

"Alright then, don't stay up too late." He kissed his head and went up.

"Goodnight."

*****

Ziro and two other members of the twelve walked into the clubhouse, with a few of his bodyguards. The guards stood inside, watching for any signs of trouble in the rowdy club. Some of the club patrons didn't seem too happy with their presence in the club, they gave them angry looks and the hostility in the room was palpable. While some even went as far as to raise their jackets displaying that they were carrying guns.

Ziro and the two other members walked into the office as they were led by some other native American looking man. They walked into a darkened corridor which led to an inner room which room which was the main office from the looks of it. The opened the door, standing outside and gesturing for them to go into the office.

"Ziro! Just the man I wanted to see." Samoa, the leader of the Nevada werewolf pack stood up as he came around his desk opening his arms and hugging Ziro along with the other two who entered behind with him. Ziro didn't know what to make of this warm reception given his reason for coming, but he received it anyway. It wasn't that they were but they weren't friends hugged either.

Samoa was also Native American, his hair was almost to his shoulders and it was streaked with some tribal beads, making him look like some kind of a Shaman. He was wearing some Japanese looking kimono with shorts leaving his chests which was covered in different tribal tattoos open. He looked like a hobo but he was a rich Hobo. The Nevada wolf pack were one of the wealthiest packs in the world and Samoa was at the helm of things.

After the introductions had been made, they settled down into their seats, the office was not too big, but had various expensive looking arts lying around giving the room a vintage look.

"I don't see the girl anywhere, Ziro, I'm guessing there's an explanation for that." Samoa cocked his head to the side, looking suspiciously at them.

"You don't expect us to bring our merchandise so early in the game now do you, Samoa. No, we came to finalize the details of our contract before moving forward, hopefully we will be done before the end of the week and head back to London before the next full moon if all goes as the plan."

"I wasn't aware we were playing a game, Ziro." Before Ziro could give him a reply there was a knock at the door and the door opened almost immediately. A young woman wearing some kind of tribal skinned skirt and bikini top walked in with a tray of drinks and settled them down on the table.

'Will that be all Samoa," she said smiling as she looked at them suggestively.

"Yes my pet, you can leave us now." Bowing ever so lightly to him, she sashayed out of the office, leaving Ziro and his mind to wonder when Samoa had even ordered the drinks but not touching it afraid it was laced with wolfsbane.

"I thought we had finalized on the terms of the contract, what more is there to talk about," Samoa said bringing them back to the conversation.

"Well for one, the money you are paying us is not nearly enough for the importance of this girl, but we're going to let that go. We want to be included in the sacrifice of the blood moon," Ziro said all this in one breath adjusting himself on his seat and trying not to show his nerves.

"We think that will be fair for all us, Samoa," one of the guy to Ziro's left added.

"That was not the contract Ziro, the agreement was that I get the girl for fifty million dollars, I think that is a fair price for a little girl, Ziro."

"That little girl is going to change your pack forever and you know it, wither agree to this or we walk and take our business elsewhere," Ziro said, bluffing.

"Now, now, Mr. Ziro, no need to throw threats around in my house, I'm sure we can come to some sort of agreement." He kept quiet for a while, not liking to be double-crossed by some greedy British assholes but concealing his anger.

"How many of you are going to be included in the sacrifice?" Samoa asked.

"We ought to be twelve, but we are ten now, the girl killed two of us," Ziro said not liking that he had to admit that she had bested them.

"Fine. Ten of you and I pay twenty five million dollars. That's my final offer." Samoa said.

"Done, you will have the girl by the end of the week," Ziro said looking at his partners who nodded at him before he faced Samoa.

Looking at his calendar Samoa said, "That will be... 28th of the month, is that right?"

"Yes."

"How about delivery, can you handle it or should I send some of my guys," looking affronted, Ziro replied him.

"We can handle her ourselves, we got her from England to the States, didn't we?"

"Well that is debatable given your last attempt." Not having any comeback for that Ziro kept his mouth shut and stoop up, his partners standing with him.

"I will transfer the funds first thing tomorrow morning as soon as you send me the account, is that alright with you?"

Ziro simply nodded his reply as they shook hands, sealing the agreement.

"My guys will show you out."
*****

Reina didn't know how long she had been in the room. The guards watched her like they were guarding the most expensive piece of art and she had not seen sunlight for only God knows how long. They brought in food for her twice a day and even though she had refused it at first for fear that it was laced with wolfsbane, two days without food began to take a toll on her and on the third day she had no choice but to eat whatever they gave her, wolfsbane or not.

She had overhead one of the guards say that they were taking her to Samoa in two days, she had no idea who the guy was but what she did know was that she didn't want to wait around to find out.

Ziro had not come to see her again after that first visit, but she knew he was near. She had also overheard this from one of the guards. Some of them treated her with fear while they came to give her, her meal, while others didn't even try to mask their disdain. They had untied the ropes from around her while she had been asleep, so she had been free to move around the room.

She had tried to look for an exit but unless she could walk through walls, there was no way out of the room. So she bided her time and waited for the first opportunity she got.

That night before they had come to carry her out, they had given her food to eat and water to drink, she knew they had laced it with a heavy dosage of sleeping drugs, so she had not touched the meal, she hid it under her bed and poured the water away laying on the floor as if she had already passed out in order to fool them.

They fell for it and carried her out, not even bothering to bind her hands or her legs. She was happy about that because that would have made her escape much more difficult. With her eyes shut tight, she felt as the lifted her and deposited her in the trunk of a car. She heard Ziro's voice just before the trunk was closed.

"Are you sure she's out of it?"

"Yes sir, I laced the food myself, the dosage I put in her water could take out a whole army," the man carrying her said.

"Good...." The trunk was shut promptly and she couldn't make out anything else they said. Opening her eyes and looking around, she was greeted with darkness as she could not even see her own fingers, using her ultra eyes, she was able to make out the things inside the trunk, there were ropes, masking tape and a crowbar. She guessed the ropes and tapes were for her but she heaved a sigh of relief at the sight of the crow bar, they must have thought she was really out of it to leave a crowbar with her.

As she made to grab it and use it to pop the trunk, she was jostled to the side making her aware that the car had started moving, not knowing how long the drive would take and not wanting to take the chance, she immediately righted herself as quietly as she could and began to use to use the crowbar to try to open the trunk. Leaving the crowbar inside the vehicle was their second mistake, they had underestimated her.

Their first mistake was not binding her hands, but it all worked to her benefit because the trunk popped open on her second attempt. Stilling herself and waiting to see if they had noticed the noise but she heard nothing. She lifted the trunk slightly and peeped out to see if they were being followed by another vehicle but the coast was clear. So she waited for the vehicle to slow down a bit, since they were driving on a rocky and isolated road the car wasn't going very fast at all.

It was now or never, making her movie as quietly as she could Reina opened the trunk wider and jumped out of the moving vehicle. She stumbled slightly on the rocky road and didn't feel anything for a second before a blinding pain shot through her arms and she gasped from the force of it. She didn't let this slow her down however, she stood up and looking around her, she dashed into surrounding woods. One of them must have seen her as she was running into the bushes because the cars stopped and the men got down and raced after her.

Reina ran like her life depended on it because it literally did, she didn't know how long she was running for, she couldn't not see anything because it was really dark but she continued to run blindly hearing the men curse loudly as they gave chase. She ran toward a particular direction and didn't why, but she knew that salvation was there.

Chapter 3

Darren just got off the phone with his friend and coworker Jackson, they had been talking about how exciting his weekend in Las Vegas was going to be.

His brother's wedding was finally here, he was happy for his little brother who had been through so much with his fiancé, Jas, he was happy that love came through for them both.

They both lived in Las Vegas, and Zack worked as a very a successful web developer for a well-known company and that was where he met Jasmine, his fiancée. They had gone through a rough patch in their almost 4 year long relationship about eight months ago, when Jasmine had lost the child she was carrying but they were able to overcome it and with some counseling, they got back on the right track and now Jas was pregnant with another child. The whole family could not be happier.

Darren himself was so happy for Zack he couldn't stop chattering about the wedding to literally all his friends back at work, it was that bad that they even sent Jas and Zack a wedding present to show their happiness for the soon to be newly married couple. He left work early at 2:00pm and went straight home. Troy was home already and had already finished packing up his stuff. So they hit the road to LAX.

"Did you get the cuff links for the other groomsmen?" Darren asked Troy who was driving, his face as stoic as always, you would think he was having an argument with the highway.

Troy smiled and glanced at him in exasperation. "Yeah, I did. I had my assistant deliver them to the house last week. The delivery guy just delivered it not long before you arrived."

Darren smiled back at him, he knew he had asked Troy this about a million times, but he just wanted to be sure everything with the wedding was going to go smoothly without any hiccup. He was glad that Troy understood him the way he did, someone else may get mad at all the questions, but not his Troy.

They got to the airport in record time and went through all the protocols before they boarded the plane. They got to Nevada in four hours. A black SUV they had already pre-hired already waiting for them at the airport to take them to Las Vegas.

The foray to Las Vegas was quite fetching as Las Vegas is a very beautiful city, but that was not what caught Darren's attention. It was Troy, his beautiful specimen of a husband who sat next on him on the ride. It's always Troy. He couldn't resist grazing Troy's fingers and taking his fingers into his own and holding them tight. Troy gaze however was still out the window as he was so captivated by the beauty of the city.

"You know I love you right?" Darren asked bringing Troy's attention to him.

Troy looked over at him now and smiled that his beautiful smirk/smile that never failed to make his heart beat faster. "I know. I love you too, babe."

"More than you will ever know." As he said this, Darren couldn't stop himself, he leaned over to kiss Troy softly on his lips.

"I love you so much." Darren whispered in his lips.

"I know... you've mentioned it before I think." Troy gave him that beautiful smirk again as he joked eliciting a slight chuckle from Darren.

They drove into Spring Valley, one of the best neighborhoods in Las Vegas.

"Zack lives here? I had no idea he moved." The confusion plain in his voice as he asked Darren.

"Yeah, he moved in recently, in preparation for the wedding. What with them starting a new family and all."

"Of course he did." Darren laughed in response.

The house was gorgeous. It looked like it belonged in a movie.

They packed in front of a ginormous mansion just as the giant mahogany front door burst open, displaying a rich looking Zack wearing a white suit and his fiancé, Jasmine in a cute yellow dress.

"There you are, shithead!! What took you so long?" Zack shouted as he came down the winding steps from the front door leading to where their car was packed.

"Work did... we're here now."

"Yes, you are, Doc. You are here."

"Hello, Troy," Zack said, strolling towards Troy.

"You look even more smashing as always."

"Hey, Zack, you look good yourself." Troy said opening his arms as Zack came to his side and hugged him.

"Marriage will do that to you, you should know." Zack laughed in reply.

Darren saw the two and asked, "Don't I get a hug too?" with a joking pout on his face.

Jasmine replied him this time coming down behind Zack. "Of course you do, Darren."

"Hello, Troy," Jasmine said reaching for him.

"Hey, Jasmine," he replied, moving into her embrace.

"I am the bride!!!!" Jasmine said jokingly showing her ring.

"Yeah, I already I knew that," Troy replied with a chuckle.

They all went inside the house chatting about California, leaving their load for the driver to bring in.

"So how's work?" Zack asked.

"Work's great. You know last week I cured a woman with Arrhythmia."

"Arrrrhhhh...what? I don't know what that is."

"It's a heart disease Zack. You need to start reading more books."

"Yeah right," Zack replied rolling his eyes.

"What about you, Troy?" Zack asked.

"What about me?"

"How's work in the firm?"

"Work's great actually, we plan on recruiting interns soon."

That sounds nice.

Jasmine chimed in. "Alright, boys, Zack will show you to your room. Dinner is almost ready."

"Hope you guys are hungry, Jasmine's food is both pulchritudinous and scrumptious."

"I'm famished."

"Good."

Zack led them upstairs. They entered a spaced lobby leading to a long hallway by the right that displayed multiple doors. Zack showed them their room, gave them their key and left. The room was the one at the far end intending to let them have their privacy. Darren unlocked the door and they let themselves in.

The room was large with a king sized bed and a roof to floor window that brought into view a beautiful garden at the back. There was a chandelier just above the bed and a nightstand with a lamp on both side of the bed.

Their things were already in the room, so they unpacked, took a quick shower together and went back down to join Zack and Jasmine.

Jasmine saw them descending the staircase as she placed the last tray of food on the table.

"You guys are right on time," she said.

"What did you cook?" Darren asked.

"Grilled steak with grilled sweet potatoes, parmesan broccoli and zucchini salad." Jasmine replied feeling so impressed with herself.

"Well I don't know what those are but I can tell they are delicious," Troy said jokingly.

"Where is Jack?" Darren asked.

"He's just at the back, he'd be joining us very soon."

"I am here, I am here," Zack said continuously as he approached the table.

"No, it's alright, we were going to start without you either way." Darren said playfully.

"Of course, you were." Zack said sarcastically.

They got seated with Zack at the head of the table, Jasmine opposite him at the other end while Troy and Darren are seated across each other.

Jasmine began dishing the food, while they made small talks.

"So, how's the web development industry, Zack?" Troy asked shoving a full fork of zucchini salad into his mouth and moaned as the taste dissolved on his tongue.

Zack replied after seeing his reaction to the food. "I told you Jasmine was a wonderful cook."

"Yeah you did." Troy replied. "This is delicious, never tasted anything quite like it.

Jasmine feeling so pleased with her handiwork replied from across the table. "Well, thank you."

Zack began discussing about the web development Troy asked about earlier. "The web development is great actually and is getting better so far. The company's been getting better contracts lately. Creating multiple site's layouts, we also got this contract we've been trying to get for a while now."

"What contract?" Darren asked with a mouthful of parmesan broccoli and steak.

"Well it has to do with programming languages and the sort, you know. Um... re-writing web design programs in a variety of computer languages like HTML, JAVA script."

"Sounds cool."

"It's huge for us actually," Zack said taking a sip of his wine. "Got the contract from a very known company in Edinburgh and Carson's intel, our biggest competition almost got the contract but it's a relief it got to us first."

"Wow ... that's really huge, well that means we have another reason to celebrate." Darren said raising his glass of wine. He continued, "To Zack and Jasmine, to love, to family and to success."

"Cheers," they replied in unison clinking their glasses.

They finished their meal chatting about shit that made no sense at all, laughed about it, made dad jokes, laughed again, they talked about their high school and college experiences, drank a lot of wine and drank some more.

After the catch up and fun, Zack and Jasmine took care of the dishes, while Troy and Darren got ready to return to their room.

"Thanks for the meal jasmine, it was great," said Troy.

"Don't think about it, you will be having more of it this weekend," she reassured him.

"Can't wait for that," Darren said walking towards her to place a kiss on her cheek, tapping Zack on the back in appreciation.

Darren and Troy retreated to their room, it wasn't hard to find as it stood out at the far end of the hallway. Troy opened the door letting Darren in first before entering the room that is more of a suite than a room.

He closed the door behind him using its locks, took a few strides and dragging Darren to himself captured Darren's lips in his, kissing him ruthless. The kiss wasn't soft this time, it was rough like there was a hunger in him, it wasn't slow either, it was fast. Troy kissed his husband like his life depended on that kiss.

He kissed Darren like he had multiple emotions; anger, love, sadness, happiness, hunger, satisfaction all at once. He brought out his tongue using it to part Darren's mouth, shoving his tongue into it like it belonged there. He took both sides of Darren's cheeks in his hand, guarding him towards the bed, never breaking the kiss. Darren's legs hit the bed making him fall onto it.

Troy watched him with pure hunger in his eyes, he climbed on top of Darren using his elbow as support just beside Darren's head. Troy began kissing him all over again, he kissed him everywhere. From lips to temples using his tongue to stroke down to Darren's throat, sucking on it hard to leave a sheen of saliva in its wake, biting slightly while Darren moaned in reaction to the sweet pain.

Darren couldn't help himself as Troy kept moving lower, ripping off his shirt to expose his bare muscled chest. He moved even lower using lips, tongue, teeth and saliva while making a mess, stopping just on the navel to make slimy circles with his tongue, Darren jerked to the contact but Troy did not stop, he knew that was Darren's weak spot.

"Uhmmmm," Darren moaned, his eyes rolling to the back of his head.

"Shhhhh," Troy replied using his tongue to smack that exact spot. Making Darren moan even louder.

Troy moved to take off Darren's pants but made Darren gasp bringing Troy to a sudden halt with his hand.

"What?" Troy asked looking up, confusion clear as day on his face.

"Ummmm, we can't have sex in brother's house," Darren replied, trying to catch his breath.

"Why not?" Troy asked already getting frustrated.

Darren replied playfully, "We could be loud you know."

"They are like a country away," Troy exaggerated.

"We won't still take chances, they could hear us and I don't want that." Darren said, trying to make Troy understand.

"Alright then, but that doesn't mean I would stop kissing you," he replied playfully as he reached up and took Darren's lips in his, sucking on it.

***

Troy woke up to find he was alone in bed, he got up and strolled to the roof to floor window to check out the garden under the bright beautiful sun. He adored the brightness of the sun. He always said, "The sun was shiny."

He went into the bathroom. It was large, with a hot bath at the far end of the room opposite the shower with a glass door. Bathrobes hung on two walls and two clean towels were neatly folded in a knitted basket on a bench sited at one side of the bathroom. A wall to wall mirror hangs just above two white sink.

A low shelf that matches bench is situated at another side of the wall for toothpaste, toothbrush, shampoo, soap and deodorants.

Troy took note of his surrounding feeling impressed. He used the toilet, took a long bath and got dressed and went downstairs to join Darren, Zack and Jasmine.

"There you are sleepyhead," Darren said after spotting.

"Morning," Troy said to Jasmine and to Zack, then walked to Darren placing a kiss on his lips. "Morning babe."

"Sleep good?" Darren asked giving him a knowing look, remembering Troy's screams as a result of his nightmare. Nightmares he always has but never agrees to share.

"Yeah I did." Troy replied going to take a sit at the dining table. Zack served Troy bacon and eggs. "Thanks, Zack."

"Yeah but I won't take all the credit, it's Jasmine's cooking."

Troy took a massive bite of the bacon and eggs. "Mmmmmm..." Troy moaned loudly.

"I don't think I've ever tasted egg this good." Hearing this, Darren looked up at Troy cocking a brow. Feeling very guilty, Troy stammered, "I- I- I mean..."

"I know what you meant, Troy." Darren said feigning an angry look.

"Well am sure Troy did not mean to hurt your feelings or insult your cooking Darren.... Jasmine chimes in playfully while Zack sat back laughed about what was happening.

"Anyway, Troy and I are going to take a look around the city. Troy has never been to Las Vegas so I am taking him out to show him how beautiful the city is." Darren explains dramatically, waving his finger in the air.

"Really? Where are you guys going?" Zack asked his brother.

"THE DREAM!" But that would be after the rehearsal dinner, of course.

***

The SUV Darren and Troy drove came to a screeching halt in front of the reception for the rehearsal dinner and Zack driving a convertible with Jasmine on the passenger seat followed right after. Already there was a Lexus and a black Jeep parked indicating Jasmine's family and Zack's father had arrived.

They got down and strolled in making small talks. Jasmine walked quicker than the others, she opened the door to reveal her family and soon to be father-in-law.

Jasmine's mom, Esma spotted her first from across the room and gasped loudly, Julian noticed her reaction and turned to see what she was looking at.

"Jasmine!!!" Julian screamed having everybody's attention.

"Hello baby sister... Guess who's getting married tomorrow." Jasmine playfully making them both laugh as Esma took long strides to meet.

"Oh my baby!!!" Esma said with tears in her eyes but they were happy tears.

"Hello mom," Jasmine replied, taking her mom's hand in hers and hugging her tightly.

Julian and Rowan joined them right after. "Hello, baby," Rowan said placing a kiss on Jasmine's head and hugging her.

"Hey dad," Jasmine replied hugging him but almost immediately breaking free to hug her sister tightly.

Zack and Darren's father moved in to congratulate the soon to be bride as well. "Thanks, William," Jasmine replied.

Zack, Darren and Troy then moved to join them, meeting William first.

"Hey dad," they said in unison.

"Hey boys," William replied hugging both of them before greeting Troy.

They all congratulated the soon to be bride and groom and headed to the table to wait the other guests. Soon after people began trooping in, Jasmine's best friend Ashley came by and other guests of the wedding and they got seated waiting for the rehearsal to begin.

After a while, caterers starting trooping in with a variety of dishes. First with pork, sliders, Mac and cheese then salad kabob all the while drinking all types of alcohol. They made jokes, chatted and made merry. Then it was time for the toast, William stood up raising his glass and clinking it with a teaspoon to get everybody's attention.

"Good morning, everyone. For those of you that don't already know who I am, I am William Moseley and I am the father of the groom. I'd like to thank everyone for joining us on the day. As I look at these beautiful people today, I think back to when Zack introduced Jasmine to me a few years back. He told me dad she's the one and I couldn't be prouder because she was selfless, spirited, beautiful and kind, and I saw why Zack fell in love with her. Now it's ridiculously hard to imagine family without her and after tomorrow, she'll officially be a Moseley. Jack, your mother, God bless her soul will be very proud of you."

"Now I don't want to hold up the rest of the celebration, so let me wind it up with a bit of advice for Zack and Jasmine. Every morning when you wake up, make a promise to yourselves to always put each other's happiness before your own."

"Congratulations and have a blessed marriage."

Claps, whistles, clinks.

Troy and Darren did not return home after the rehearsal dinner. Just as Darren promised Troy, he was taking him to see the city. Darren got into the driver seat with Troy in the passenger seat and drove away into the city.

"Hey," Darren said taking a glance at Troy.

"Hey," Troy said back without turning around trying to conceal his worry.

Darren knowing what was on his mind said. "You had that nightmare again."

"Darren, I- I- I..."

Darren cut him off saying, "I know. You will tell me when you can, am not pushing. I just want you quit thinking about it, it's affecting us. It's like that nightmare is taking you away from me."

With this, Troy turns to face him; "Nothing can ever take me away from you and am sorry making you feel that way."

"Promise?"

"I promise baby." Troy replied, reassuring him.... "I love you so much."

"I know." Darren smiled, never taking his eyes off the road.

*****

THE DREAM

They got to the south east end of The Dream, where the Marbella bay hotel/resort is located. They parked the vehicle in the parking lot and strolled the rest of the way, entering the resort.

"Wow," Troy said turning a complete 360 degrees to take in the whole view.

"I know," Darren replied. Then led him towards the aquarium to watch the beautiful display of sharks, fish, reptiles, and marine vertebrates that were all on display.

They walked around for a while, holding hands and watching every kind of sea animal there was to see. After the aquarium, they left the resort and strolled round the streets to the Chancery hotel and took the Gondola rides.

They got two tickets for the boat ride and got in. The gondola ride was a quick one going through a man-made Italian village full of quaint shops with neon lights making it even more beautiful. They both watched the sunset under the darkening blue sky while the ride ended. They got off the boat and headed to Cleopatra's palace right in the middle of the dream. It was completely dark now and the city was lit with neon lights as they stood close to the waterfall.

"Wow," Troy said astonished. "I wish I grew up here."

"Everybody says that," Darren replied.

"How many people have you brought here?" Troy asked in a forced jealous tone.

"Just you, baby," Darren said as he leaned in to kiss him softly, parting his lips and shoving his tongue into Troy's lips like it belonged there. Well it did, didn't it?

Troy kissed him back passionately, sucking on his tongue. They both got carried away kissing and moaning in each other's mouth but Darren recovered first breaking the kiss, releasing a breath he didn't realize he was holding.

They left Cleopatra's palace and took a stroll to Mydas Hotel loving the ancient Egyptian theme design. The hotel was shaped like a giant diamond with a lion proudly gazing out over the street.

That was about it, after they had seen almost every building and resort in the dream they went back to the parking lot where their rental car sat, got in and hit the road back to Zack's house.

"Are you gonna keep staring at me or do you want to say something?" Darren asked noticing Troy's piercing gaze.

"Well, I don't want to say anything, I just can't stop staring at you that's all," Troy said, meaning it.

Darren became speechless straight off, that's what Troy always did to him. He always made him speechless.

Troy saw the effect he had on Darren and smiled. The effect he always has Darren.

The drive back to Zack's house was short. Darren parked the car in the garage, they both got down. They entered the house to find Zack walking down the staircase already dressed in a blue shirt, leather jacket and black trouser with matching boots.

"There you guys are... " Zack said adjusting his collar as he came to a stop at the end of the staircase. "What took you so long?"

"We went to the dream like I told you and we had to see a lot of places, you know how it works at the dream," Darren said feeling so pleased he could see the strip with his husband.

"Yeah, I know, great place," Zack said remembering his experience at the strip with Jas.

"Where's Jasmine, by the way?"

"She left for her bachelorette party."

"Shit, we are supposed to be at your bachelor party," Darren said regretfully.

"Yup," Zack said without judgement. "You guys go get ready. We have thirty minutes left."

With that they went up to their room, took a quick shower and got dressed. Troy was dressed in a white shirt that showcased his biceps when he flexed his muscles, black crazy jean and a denim jacket that matched his massive boots, giving him the look of a college football player.

"You look so hot," Darren said, eyeing him from head to feet.

"Yeah?" Troy replied smacking his ass. That made Darren yelp in surprise.

They went back down to join Zack and a few friends that had arrived.

"Hey guys, this is Tim and this is Josh. They will be joining us," Zack said as he introduced the guys.

They drove to a strip club downtown coming to a halt in the parking area filled with cars indicating the other guys joining them had arrived and waiting.

They entered the club to be welcomed by a burst of music, screams and weird noises coming from different booths. Zack spotted his friends from the other corner of the room and led Darren, Troy and the others towards them. They squeezed through the crowd, rubbing off drunk sweaty bodied dancers, they made way using their hands to clear a path for themselves. They reached their booth finally meeting the half-drunk friends.

"Hey!" Zack screamed through the loud music to be heard as his friends stood up give a hug each.

Darren, so tired of being sober waved a waitress over to order their shots. They drank and drank and kept it coming, rounds and rounds. They finally took a pause to propose that Zack went up the stage for a lap dance by one of the strippers.

"No, no, no, no, no...." Zack kept saying shying away from the proposal but exasperated Troy couldn't deal with that. He got up and climbed the stage collecting a mic.

"No, no, no... wh... what the fuck is he doing?" Zack asked in horror.

"Ahem... can I get everyone's attention please?" Troy asked from the stage. "So tomorrow is my buddy's wedding and we are throwing him a bachelor's party. We've made a proposal though, he's going to be joining me right now on stage for a lap dance, so get him a stool and a dancer, if you would please."

The crowd goes wild. "Zack... Zack... Zack!" Calling repeatedly.

"You got it, buddy," Darren said patting his back.

"Asshole," he replied with a grin.

Having no choice, he got up and walked to the stage that already had a stool waiting for him squeezing through the crowd of sweaty bodies. Troy watched as he climbed the stage and sank into the stool like that could save him. After a moment, a dancer wearing a thong and a bikini bra walked towards him slowly, trying to look seductive.

Moving one leg over his, she sat down on his lap straddling him. She began moving her hips, slowly at first then in a swift move she turned so her back was to. She danced on his laps, rolling her hips, moving back and forth. When she satisfied with the hips work, she got up to face him giving him a cocky smile as she raised a leg, placing it on his shoulder bringing him too close to him.

"That girl can dance," Troy said to Darren at the booth.

"She's good at it," Darren replied. "That thing she did with her leg... the leg thing, that was so sexy. Jas would kill him if she was here."

"I know," Troy said amused that Darren took notice of a sexy woman given the fact that he was gay.

The girl from the stage never stopped, she kept dancing on Zack, behind him, all over him showing off her tits, wriggling them right on his face. Zack had relaxed into the dance because the shots he had been given were starting to kick in. Just as he about was about to grab her waist, she pulled back.

"That's about enough dance for you, lover boy," she said to Zack walking away making him groan at the loss of contact.

Troy and Darren left the booth to get Zack out of the stage and to the section for games. They played pool pong and a few other games before heading back home to get some rest before the wedding.

***

It was finally Darren's brother's wedding. Darren had never seen Zack so happy and anxious. They were all at the wedding gathering, Darren's father, Jasmine's family, friends, guests from different parts of the country all waiting for the bride to walk down the aisle. Darren stood next to his brother at the altar as his best man reassuring him everything would be fine cos Zack was so tensed and anxious.

Darren went back to stand with Troy as Jasmine finally walked down the aisle with her father, she exchanged vows with Zack and they became husband and wife.

"They are so beautiful, aren't they?" Darren said to Troy as they said their vows to each other.

"Yeah," Troy replied slowly leaning close to kiss his husband, remembering their wedding like it was yesterday

"You're so beautiful," Troy said into Darren's lips kissing him one more time before taking his attention back to the wedding.

It was time for the reception and everybody was gathered in the reception room taking the seat that had their names on them. Troy and Darren were seated in the Bride and groom's table as close family as the dishes were served and wine of the sort. The room was rowdy with people and noisy from the rain that had just started falling and thunder clapped through the sky.

Darren stood up, clinking his glass with a tea spoon to get everyone's attention. "I want to make a toast to the new wedded couple, Zack and Jasmine."

"You guys have been through a lot together and would probably still go through a lot more but as long as you have each other and you continue to put each other's happiness' before your own, you'd cross the seven seas on foot."

The rest of the families and friends made their toasts, Zack made a toast to his wife expressing his love.

The reception was almost over when Darren got a call from work telling him he had to be back as soon as possible, his patient he left back at the hospital before had just died and he had to return at once.

Troy noticed Darren's tension and walked over to him. "Everything alright, Darren?"

Darren turned with a startled look to face his husband. "We've gotta go, now!!!" Darren replied still filled with terror.

"What's the matter Darren?" Troy asked filled with worry.

"My patient just died," Darren said unable to hide his pain

They both went to search for Zack and Jas telling them they were sorry but they had to leave. Zack nodded in understanding offering to give them a ride to the airport but they refused because he could not leave his own wedding.

Troy and Darren went back to their rooms to pack up and leave, Troy tried to book a flight while Darren packed all their things.

"Hey babe, I can't book a flight, all flights have been grounded due to the heavy rain." Troy said feeling sorry for his husband still having a meltdown.

"Um.... Ok, we could drive back, I don't care. I just need to get back to the hospital," Darren said not thinking anymore. They both went to Zack asking to borrow one of his cars. He gave them the keys and bade them goodbye.

They drove into the storm, Troy insisted he took the wheel because Darren wasn't up for a drive through the storm with so much going through his mind. As they were leaving Nevada, Troy spotted something in the middle of the road. No, not something....someone.

Chapter 4

Troy stepped on the brake bringing the car to a screeching stop a few inches from the woman. Darren who wasn't paying any attention as his focus was outside his window turned in shock to clarify what had happened. A naked and badly injured woman lay in the middle of the road with her hair as dark as the night. Troy immediately recognized the smell of wolf's bane on her realizing she was like him.

While Darren saw pain, hurt and a vulnerable woman, Troy saw a darkness, danger, and a threat to the secret he had kept tucked away from the world and his Darren. He has not seen a wolf in years and he didn't want to be around this one, he steps on the brake for a second time but this time, he drove off.

"Call 911," Troy said to Darren driving past the woman.

"We can't just leave her here, she could die," Darren said fumbling with his phone.

"Yes, so call 911."

"No service, we have to go back."

Troy hesitatingly turned the car around, driving back to where the women laid. Darren got down from the vehicle before it was stopped, running to the women already passed out, using his jacket to cover her nudity.

"She's still alive!" Darren called out finding a pulse. "We have to take her to the hospital."

"What? We can't take her, we don't even know who she is," Troy said defensively, keeping his distance because of the wolf's bane on her. "Troy, look at her, she will die if we leave her here and 911 isn't going through."

"Alright," Troy said in frustration.

Darren carried the woman to the back seat and they drove straight to the closest hospital they could find. Throughout the way, Troy tried to distract himself from the wolf's bane on her driving above speed limits. As got to the hospital, Troy got down the car maintaining a good distance from the woman while Darren tried to dress the woman with one of his clothes that swallowed the her whole.

They both entered the hospital, Darren carrying the woman and screaming at everybody he met on the corridor kept telling himself that he couldn't save his patient back at home but he would save this one. Some doctors came running towards them to carry the woman to the accident and emergency ward.

After a while a doctor walked up to them telling them she was alright and she had sustained only bruises, but she was fine and almost ready to go back home. Troy and Darren both went into the ward to see the woman already awake and seated.

"Who are you?" she asked

"We are the guys that saved your life," Troy replied with an attitude.

Darren ignored him, walking towards the woman. "Hey, I'm Darren and this is my husband, Troy."

"How did I get here?" she asked looking round like she didn't know what a hospital looked.

"We saw you on the road naked and injured, we couldn't leave you." Darren answered.

"Can you tell us your name?" Troy asked, his patience starting to wear out.

"Reina," she answered, even though she was curious as to why he seemed to hate her when he didn't even know her.

Troy got curious and strolled towards her. He stopped at a reasonable distance but close enough to startle her, bringing the massive shirt she wore down her shoulders.

That's when Troy noticed it. He did not understand it at first but then he remembered. The tattoo on her shoulder, the same one he always saw in his dreams, the same similar tattoo he had on his own shoulder. He stood in shook for a moment, thinking to himself. "Was it possible?"

All of a sudden the room became too small, he had to get out of there but he also needed answers. However he had to wait, he couldn't risk Darren finding out anything about the secret.

"Are you ok, Troy?" Darren asked.

"Yeah, I'm fine."

Darren was not convinced but he dropped it knowing not to push any further. While Reina just stared at Troy having the same suspicions.

"Where do we drop you off?" Troy asked not taking his eyes off her.

What state is this?" Reina asked.

"You don't know where you are?" Troy asked very confused.

"No... I was kidnapped and taken to Nevada but I escaped and that's how you found me," she replied.

"You are in LA, California," Troy said looking at her like he could read her.

Reina sighed by the sound of that feeling so relieved she was no longer with her captors, but she could not trust anybody, she could not let her guard down again.

"Do you have a place, at least somewhere we can drop you off when you get discharged?"

"No," she replied.

"So, where do we drop you off?" Troy asked starting to lose his patience.

"I don't know," she replied. "I've never been in California. I don't even know anybody here."

"You can follow us back home, stay with us until you can get back on your feet." Darren said, not considering Troy's opinion.

"What? ...No, she can't follow us back home." Troy said to his husband.

Darren turned to Troy saying; "So what do you suggest Troy, we just abandon her?"

"We take her to where we found her. Oh, got I've a better idea, we take her to the cops Darren, that is what I suggest."

"Don't take me to the cops please..." Reina cried.

"Can we talk outside?" Troy said to Darren pulling him outside the room.

"Babe, we have to take her home. I mean, look at her," Darren said pointing at the door.

"I know but we don't even know who she is or why she was kidnapped in the first place. She could be trouble," Troy replied feeling very frustrated, he didn't want to get involved with a were wolf and he was one hundred percent sure that Reina was one, probably from his pack in New Orleans. but Darren was right and if he was going to get any answers about his nightmares, she was his best bet.

Besides he wanted to know why she was kidnapped and what she was doing so far from home. New Orleans wolves rarely ever left their state, he had to hear her story.

"We have to help her," Darren said, hoping Troy would change his mind.

"Why can't we just take her to the cops?" Troy asked adamantly.

"Because she needs our help not the cop. She could be traumatized or worse, I want to help her. We need to help her, Troy."

"Alright, but if we are keeping she never leaves our sight. We keep her close, always," Troy said finally giving in.

"That won't be a problem," Darren said relieved as they went back to the room.

"You're coming with us but that's just because my husband is a doctor and he wants to make sure you're really fine," Troy said to Reina showing he was obviously not ok with that.

"Thank you," Reina said looking at Darren before turning to face Troy.

"Alright, I'm going to get the doctor so we can check YOU out," Darren said as he left the room.

"Am sorry, I did not mean to cause you any trouble," Reina said to Troy.

"That ship has sailed, wrecked and sank. We are fucking way past that, bringing you here to the hospital is already a hand full but we're fucking taking you home. You don't think that's enough trouble?" Troy said furiously.

"I know. I am sorry," Reina replied.

Troy ignored her this time, he was completely frustrated. He turned a full 360 as he combed through his with his fingers. Although he was so angry, he could not avoid the voice in his head that said it was fate that brought Reina to him. Meeting the girl with the tattoo, the tattoo that haunted in his dreams, but he did not believe in fate or destiny. He needed answers.

Darren came into the room with a burger in his hand for Reina and a doctor carrying a notepad, the doctor check Reina's vitals once again and discharged her. The three of them walked down the hall to the receptionist to check out of the hospital. Troy took longer and faster strides reaching the car first, it was past dawn already and all he wanted was to get back home and wash the night off. The drive home was very quiet and that relieved because he was ready for a conversation with anybody, not even Darren.

They got home, Darren showed her the guest room and gave her some blankets and clean towels while Troy took their things to their room.

"You hungry?" Darren asked Reina.

"Yeah, I am," she replied feeling a little shy and embarrassed at the sound of her belly growling.

"Alright, I'm going to order some takeout."
**

As Darren left the room, Reina slumped on the floor and began to cry. She cried out of frustration, relief, anger or just because of the fact that she was safe and no longer with her captors. After a while of crying and thinking to herself, she got up and went to the bathroom to take a very long shower. The bathroom already had all she needed, shampoo, toothpaste, a new toothbrush and lavender soap. It was like they knew she was coming. She put on the shower and let hot water scald her skin like she wanted to shred it off, she wanted a new skin after what they did to her back in Nevada. After the shower, she crawled into bed and fell asleep immediately.

Reina ran through the woods screaming, but this time was different. This time, she was running with somebody. She could not make out the person's features or looks but she was certain it was a man, a man she recognized. Ziro and his men were closing in on them but they never caught up with them. It was like this man was her guardian angel. He protected her as they ran out of the woods together and into the road. She recognized this road, she did not know how or why but she did.

Reina woke up with a start, it took her a few moments to remember where she was and how she got there, her face was pouring with sweat and her clothes were soaked in it. She looked around her, feeling someone else's presence in the room and found the figure of Troy standing very still by the door, still as a statue and watching her in the dark. His eyes were almost glowing but she could not be sure.

She wondered why he stood there and almost immediately her thoughts went back to the dream she had been having. It felt like she was always drawn to him, whenever he was near she felt a certain connection she could not explain. Back in Nevada, she had been drawn to that particular road where they had met her, and now, she dreamt about it while he was in the room.

When he still stood there saying nothing, she spoke first. "What are you doing here?"

"This is my house," he replied her.

"You were having a nightmare," he said suspiciously, trying to read her thoughts.

"That is what people do when they sleep, is it not?" she asked with sarcasm.

"Your food is getting cold in the kitchen," he replied ignoring her sarcasm and left the room before she could ask where the kitchen was.

She got up immediately following him downstairs and the kitchen. She could not help turning round to take in the beauty of the house. Paintings hung on the walls, family pictures and pictures of Troy and Darren together. The touched them one by one as she descends the staircase with Troy in front of her but paying no attention to what she was doing. She thought the house was beautiful as she had never been anywhere as beautiful.

"Like what you see?" Troy asked her bringing her out of her thoughts.

"It's beautiful," she admitted.

Troy led her into the kitchen to join Darren seated on a stool, almost done with his food. He stood as he noticed their arrival.

"You were in there for a while," Darren said to her with a smile as he walked up to both of them.

"I was asleep, I did not mean to wake you guys wait." she replied.

"It's ok, you needed the sleep. Hope you are hungry though." Darren said playfully, trying not to scare her away.

"Yeah, I am," she replied.

"Good," he said as he served her pasta in a plate and passed it to her.

She took the plate and devoured the food like an animal, regardless of Troy and Darren watching her like she was a creep. She looked up, noticing both Troy and Darren staring at her eating habit and took a pause.

"I'm sorry, I haven't eaten anything this good in a while," she said sheepishly and tried to eat normally.

"That's fine." Darren assures her pouring more pasta in her plate and placing a bottle of water beside her.

She finished eating the food and downed the water, emptying the bottle in an instant. She cleaned her mouth with the robe she was wearing as she had nothing else to wear.

"I know you have questions, how I got on the road and why I was kidnapped but I really don't have any answer, I really don't know what happened," she said turning to face Troy.

"Bullshit!" Troy snapped, calling her out on her lie and startling Darren.

"What is the problem, Troy?" Darren asked confused.

"Tell me you don't believe what she says, Darren," he said.

"Yeah, well can you give her a break? She just got here and you are scaring her. She could be traumatized," Darren said. Troy just walked out of the kitchen, going straight to his room.

"I am sorry if I am causing any trouble," Reina said, actually feeling bad for the both of them.

"No. I am sorry for his behavior," Darren replied. "You should go to your room."

"Thanks for the meal. It was really great," she said as stood up to leave.

"Goodnight, Reina."

She went back to her room following the same route she and Troy came from earlier. She entered the room and crawled into bed feeling a little better as she had rested, cleaned up and eaten but she could not stop thinking about her dream. The mystery man that saved her, the road and Troy. She fell asleep thinking of her dream and Troy who she sensed was just like her and also from her pack.

***

Darren got back home with a few clothes for Reina and took it to her room. He entered the after knocking once on the door to find Reina standing by the window.

"Hey," he said, drawing her attention to him.

"Hi," she said, turning around to face him.

"I... uh, I got a few clothes from the mall for you." He handed it to her.

"Thank you," she replied as she looked into the bag.

"I did not know your size of clothes so I got what I thought would fit."

"It's alright. Thanks a lot, Darren. I owe you guys my life." She smiled.

"Sure. You know you can talk to me about anything right?" He asked her, trying to relax her into his home. "About the kidnapping, if you have trouble sleeping or you are stressed, you can come to me. I still think we should call the cops but I will respect your wishes not to."

"I know... thank you. I don't think the cops would be of much help and I promise I'm not a serial killer or anything like that," she whispered more to herself than him.

"Alright then, I will go make dinner." With that, Darren left the room and went to the kitchen to join Troy already preparing the food.

"Are you ok?" Darren asked Troy sensing his mood.

"Why do you trust the girl so much," Troy asked dropping what he was doing.

"Reina, her name is Reina, Troy. And I don't trust her, I am helping her," he replied, his patience wearing thin.

"Then why are you helping her? You don't trust her, we don't know her. Why can't we just take her to the cops?

"Because I could not save Emma but I can save Reina," he snapped. Talking about his patient that died while he was away hurt him so bad because he became close with her while he treated in the hospital.

"Baby, Emma's death was not your fault," Troy said, realizing why Darren felt so obligated to save Reina.

"But it was. It was my fault, if only I had been around maybe I could have saved her," he replied Troy almost in tears.

"You can't keep blaming yourself for what happened, Darren. You were at your brother's wedding, you could not have known." Troy tried to convince him.

"I think that is the problem, that I did not know she was going to die is the problem," he said at the verge of tears.

Troy walked to him and hugged him tightly, giving him comfort he needed as he cried on his shoulders. This was the first time Darren lost a patient that he could have saved. He was having a severe meltdown and Troy was not sure if he could help him out of it.

"It was not your fault baby, stop blaming yourself. It was not your fault," Troy said in a whisper trying to reassure him.

"I should have been there. I should have been able to save her," Darren replied adamantly. "That is why I feel this strong urge to save Reina. I feel like she was there for a reason. I could not save Emily but I have been given a chance to make up for that." But Troy knows better.

"Well if you say it's your fault, then it is also my fault," Troy said trying to share in his pain.

"What are you talking about? You were not her doctor."

"No. I was not her doctor but I was there with you, at the wedding," Troy said to him with a smile.

"Don't try to take the blame, Troy," he said sniffing in Troy's scent.

Troy pulled him out of his embrace, took his cheeks in his palm and said, "Don't either. Emily's death was not your fault."

"Ok," he finally agreed. "I love you, Troy."

"Who doesn't?" Troy asked jokingly.

After the sentimental exchange of words, they continued cooking in silence. When the food was ready, Darren went up to Reina's room and called her down to the dining room, served her food and went back to his chair to eat. They ate in silence but Reina was well aware of Troy shooting daggers at her.

If eyes could kill, Reina was surely dead. But she did not respond, mostly because she did not know what to do but also because of Darren. She had heard the argument from earlier and she did not want to break his heart by causing a scene with Troy.

It was going to take Troy a while to trust her, if it would happen at all, she thought to herself. But how long was she going to stay? It was just a matter of time before Ziro and the 12 found her and even if Darren wants to help her now, he would not be able to help her when she was faced with Ziro, only Troy could help her.

If her suspicions were correct. But looking at things from his side, he only wanted her gone like he did not want anything to do with her. She also suspected Darren had no idea that he was a werewolf and he intended to keep it that way. She finished her meal and took her plate to the sink, turning on the tap to wash them.

"You don't have to do that," Darren said to her standing up from his chair.

"I want to, please," she replied looking back at the both of them as Troy rolled his eyes.

Darren sits back down and allowed her do her dishes but he still was not ok with it. He continued his meal, making small talks with Troy. But Troy kept staring at her trying to read her thoughts, paying less attention to Darren.

"Thank you both for the meal, and the clothes.... they fit just fine." She smiled at both of them.

"You're welcome."

"I don't want to bother you but can I get a notepad and a pen please?"

"Sure, I bring it to you tomorrow morning before work."

"Thanks."

Darren watched her as she retreated to her room, noticing Troy's irritated gazes. "Why do you hate her so much?" he asked Troy as Reina disappeared into the hallway.

"I don't hate her, I just don't trust her."

"What does that even mean?" he asked as he scoffed.

"It means she could be anybody, a thief or a psychopath. I mean, we found her naked on the road."

"That does not make her a psychopath, it means she was attacked, a victim."

"Yes of course, but how would we know that. She is not telling you anything."

Darren walked over to Troy closing their distance and kissed him, trying to shut him up before he said something else.

"Did you just shut me up?" Troy asked, smiling into Darren's lips.

"Enough talking for one day," he replied, deepening the kiss.

Troy parted his lips with his tongue driving him wild. They kiss more wildly. It was like he was being kissed from the inside out. Troy sucked on his tongue, sending shivers of desire through him like lightning bolts crashing. He could feel Troy everywhere. His heat, his mouth, his tongue.

The taste of Troy's tongue drove him to the verge of shattering to pieces, he tasted of wine which built a sweet sensation he had never felt before. Troy held him firm by the waist like he knew that if he lets go, Darren would fall to the ground.

Troy's mouth tore free from Darren's for a second but enough to draw air before returning them. Darren's moans fill the room as Troy's lips travel from his mouth to his temples and his throat, ripping off his shirt but never losing contact. He was rough but gentle at the same time.

"Touch me," Troy said.

Darren did as he said, tearing open his fly and shoving his fingers into his boxer briefs, pumping and squeezing as they moved in unison towards the table pushing off the chairs, plates and cutleries out of the way.

***

Reina could not fall asleep because of the noise coming from the dining room, she kept tossing and turning. The moans were so distressing, it took every shred of muscle in her to stay put and cover her ears with her pillow, not that it helped much. So she made up scenarios of her killing Ziro and his men, drifting off to sleep at the thought of them bleeding out at her feet.

She did not want to kill them but she had no choice, they begged and begged for their lives but she could not set them free. They would only come for her again and after what they did to her, they did not deserve forgiveness. Reina stood in front of Ziro, his men and her parents crouched down on their knees. Her parents could not look up at her, they did not see themselves worthy after selling her to murderers, so they pleaded for a quick death.

Reina granted them their wish. She slit their throats on the spot, splashing blood all over her face. She turned around unable to look at what she had done but when she looked back at them, she was horrified at what she saw. Troy and Darren lay on the floor lifeless in a pool of their own blood. She screamed loud, throwing away the knife as she dropped to the floor crying. She had their blood in her hands.

Reina woke up in shock, looking around and then looking down at her hand in search for blood, she felt relieved when she saw her hand was clean. She was dripping in sweat, and exhausted like she just ran a marathon. She bent her head, taking them in her hands just as she spotted an object by the side of her the bed. It was the notepad she had requested for last night with a pen attached to it by the side.

She smiled at the kind gesture, Darren had been nothing but good to her since they saved her, he gave her everything she needed and even though Troy was not as kind, he had not thrown her out yet. She understood his hostility, not everything was as it seems. She lived that life. After trusting Ziro and got betrayed, she was never trusting anybody ever again.

She got up from the bed and strolled to the bathroom, brushed her teeth and took a quick shower. Intending to look nice as it had been a while, she wore one of the dresses Darren got her and went downstairs for breakfast.

"You look nice," Darren said with a cup of in his hand, handing her another one.

"Thanks," she replied, reaching out to accept it. "Where is Troy?"

"He is at work. He had an early call."

"Oh!"

"You know you don't need to be afraid of Troy. He's a good man he just doesn't trust easily. You are not the problem."

"Give him time to get to know you, I'm sure you guys will become friends in no time."

"How long can I stay?"

"As long as you need."

"I have nobody to call and nowhere to go. I don't want to impose or make you guys uncomfortable, but I really have nowhere to go," she said almost in tears.

"It's ok. You can stay for as long you need, I promise."

"Thanks a lot, Darren," she said as she sipped her coffee. "Wow! This tastes amazing."

"I made breakfast, I'm sure you would be hungry."

She went into the dining room taking a seat while Darren went into the kitchen to get the food. He served it in her plate as he sat across from her on the table.

"I saw the notepad you dropped on my bed, thanks."

"You are welcome."

***

Reina has been in Troy and Darren's home for two weeks now but she was still terrified of leaving the house. Ziro and his men were still out there and they could show up anytime, she could not risk getting caught, but also Darren and Troy's lives would be in danger. If Ziro ever found out someone was protecting her, he would hunt them down and kill them. She could not let that happen.

"You always stand there, like you are searching for something... or someone," Troy said.

"I did not hear you come in," Reina replied in a startle, like she was caught off guard.

"Yeah, I knocked but there was no reply. Looks like you were lost in what you were searching for."

"I have just being off the edge since you guys saved me. I was kidnapped and even if I am safe now, I still feel like someone is going to sneak up on me anytime." She tried to explain herself, hoping Troy would change how he felt about her.

"We saved you in Nevada but you think somebody would sneak up on you here in California, in our home?"

"I know you don't understand but I am telling the truth."

"Yes, I don't understand why you don't have any family. I don't understand why you were kidnapped, I don't understand that tattoo on your shoulder and I don't understand why you have so many secrets and won't even tell us after we saved you."

"I am not keeping any secrets and I don't know why I was kidnapped," she lied but she knew Troy would never believe her.

"BULLSHIT!!! I know you are keeping secrets from us and you may have Darren fooled but you will never fool me," he said closing the distance between them, intimidating her.

"I am not fooling anybody."

"Whatever it is, I am going to find it out and you will stay out of my way. Are we clear?"

"Crystal," she said as he storms off.

She slumped on the bed heaving out the breath she didn't even know she had been saving. She had no idea how long she could go without actually telling them the truth, but she was going to stretch out for as long as she could. Trying her best to ignore her fears, she went downstairs to the kitchen intending on cooking dinner. It had been a really long time since she did something with her hands.

"What are you doing?" Troy asked startling her.

"I wanted to cook dinner. Is that ok?"

"Whatever."

"You said something about my tattoo. You don't like tattoos?" she asked as she chopped the carrots.

"I don't hate tattoos," he replied, without giving her a glance.

"Then what is wrong with mine, or is it just me you hate? She asked but he just ignores her so she continues. Why do you hate me so much?"

"We've gone over this before."

Feeling so hurt and embarrassed, she continues cooking and ignores his presence like she should have done earlier. They eat together in silence as Darren was having a late shift and wasn't going to home till the next morning. She wished Darren was there with them, at least things would not have been so awkward. After their dinner, she went up to her room and crawled into bed with whatever pride she had left, drifting to sleep.

She woke up to the sound of a knock on the door, she was getting used to waking up in a room that smelled of perfume as she no longer turns around with a racing heart to remember how she got there. The door opened to reveal Darren standing in a dress shirt and khakis as if he had not just returned from work.

"Good morning," he said to her as he entered into the room completely.

"Good morning," she replied yawning and stretching.

"Did you sleep well?" he continued as she nodded. "Am going to the mall later today, I want you to come with me, maybe shop for new clothes as well."

"Sure, I would love to come. That's so nice of you."

"Great."

Reina was too carried away by the idea of leaving the house and going shopping, forgetting Ziro was still out there, he could be anywhere and she knew that too well. They left the house using Darren's car and drove off, she stuck her head out the window during the drive feeling the fresh air, like she had forgotten what it felt like. Darren took notice of it and smiled, happy that he was making her feel good.

The car came to a stop in front of the mall and as they came down from the car and walked in, the mall was filled with people walking around and going about their business. Reina could not help the feeling of being watched, she took notice of everybody and everything around her, and anybody that walked closed to them. Darren noticed jumpiness and held her, trying his best to calm her down.

"It's ok. You are safe now, they can't hurt you anymore." Darren reassured her but she knew better.

Chapter 5

Reina tried to calm down as she and Darren walked around the massive mall. There were a lot of things to see and she couldn't help but feel amazed by the lives of the people around her. She would give anything to be like them, living without fear that somebody would one day snatch that freedom from you.

Always looking behind your shoulder and living life but not fully living. Sure they had their everyday mundane problems like work, kids or mortgage, but she would gladly exchange her problems for theirs in a heartbeat. Almost all her life she had known she was different although she didn't tell anyone, and then when she had transformed at 18 she could no longer hide it from everyone. That was almost 8 years ago, she was 26 now and she had no friends, no family and no boyfriend, nothing of the sort.

The boy she had been seeing when she was with Ziro, before he revealed his true colors had only been using her to get information to report to Ziro. She had thought herself in love with them, he was her first kiss and first everything, but he was just using her. She knew she couldn't trust anyone, not even Darren, and Troy was right in not trusting her, she just needed a little more time to figure out her next move.

She was thinking of moving to Arizona, she had nobody there but she could start afresh some place nobody knew her, maybe she could ask Darren for a loan from Darren and then pay him back when she was back on her feet. She had researched about their wolf community and they were the nicest. So at least she would try as much as possible to stay off the radar.

"Reina, Reina."

"Oh, yeah? Sorry I zoned off there for a minute." Darren had been calling her and she was so deep in thoughts she hadn't even though she hadn't even heard him. They sat across each other in one of the stalls in the mall and had gotten frozen yogurt.

"Seems like you have a lot on your mind," Darren asked, a look of concern on his face.

"You weren't rude. You're allowed to think and I really think you should stop apologizing to me or to Troy either. It wasn't your fault you got kidnapped, you're the victim here and you shouldn't be apologizing for anything." Reina was almost in tears but she blinked them back.

"Thank you, Darren, you don't know how much I needed to hear that... that it wasn't my fault."

"It isn't, just take all the time you need. Troy will come around so don't worry about him, and whatever you decide to do, you have my support one hundred percent."

"Thank you, Darren, thank you so much," she replied with a little smile.

"It's alright. What do you say we hit the boutiques and have you looking like Kendall Jenner at a Paris Fashion Show."

Laughing and getting up from where she sat, she had no idea who Kendall Jenner was so she asked him.

"Who's Kendall Jenner?" she asking unable to hide her confusion.

"Uhmm..." Darren gasped, holding his chest in mock horror. "Is that a joke? Were you even born in this generation? Not knowing the Kardashians should legit be a crime in this town."

Reina only shook her head and laughed at his antics, as they walked to a Macy's boutique. "I have no idea what you're talking about."

"Well, let's get you some clothes first then we have some keeping up to do."

. . . . .

Troy was on a video call on his laptop with some of his clients from Japan, they were talking about plans on marketing their new android smart phone and trying to infiltrate the U.S. market. His firm was in charge of publicity and advertising for the product. He was on the living room couch while they talked about cost and profit analysis and demand and supply, when he heard two familiar voices coming from outside and getting closer.

Suddenly, the sitting room door burst open as Reina and Darren walked in, carrying different shapes and sizes of shopping bags and talking over each other's voices making a ruckus.

"Oh my God, that was so hilarious! Did you watch the one about the cat humping the kitchen table." Another shout of laughter from the both of them. They were still oblivious to Troy as he watched them like they had grown horns, the shock very much visible on his face.

Pleading with his clients and asking to be excused, he logged out of the video call and shut down his laptop, the sound of it snapping shut must have captured their attention because they both stopped laughing almost immediately and looked in to see him sitting there and watching them, his face hard as stone.

"Anyone care to explain to me what the hell is happening here?" Troy asked, his voice dangerously low

"Oh, you're home," Darren spoke as if he was disappointed to see him there while Reina simply cowered behind him trying to hide the shopping bags like he hadn't already seen them.

"Oh yeah... so sorry about that, babe. I didn't get your missed calls until later, but Reina and I had fun. We went shopping and you would not believe who I saw today."

"You don't say," Troy replied dryly.

Walking further into the room with Reina trailing silently behind him, they deposited their goods on the couch but Reina thinks better of it and decides to go up with hers not wanting to be included in their fight even if she was the reason for said fight, she knew her presence would only serve to aggravate Troy.

Darren went closer to kiss him on the lips, but he did not even respond.

"How was your meeting with the Japanese people," Darren asked ignoring the angry look on his face.

"It went well," was his clipped reply.

"I was in the middle of it before I was rudely interrupted actually," he said not hiding the fact that he was talking about Reina.

"I'm so sorry, baby, I had no idea you were home," he pouted jokingly.

"It's alright."

"Are you sure?"

"Yeah."

"Okay. Well I'm just going to go get started on dinner, I might get called in today at the hospital, they are currently short staffed and need more hands on deck." He walked off, leaving Troy sitting there and stewing over his anger. Darren goes into the kitchen to start dinner but Troy stopped into.

But Troy followed, not backing down, "Now you're buying her clothes? What are you, her sugar daddy?"

"Really, Troy, we are still doing this?" Darren asked, not hiding the exasperation in his voice as he started prepping to make dinner.

"Yes, Darren, we are doing this. We don't even know who she is. We could be harboring a terrorist for all I know and you're going to buy her expensive clothes!" He gestured to the shopping bags Darren still had in the living room. His voice increasing in anger with each word he uttered.

"Oh my God, T, stop with this already, Reina was kidnapped! She was kidnapped and you hear her having nightmares almost every night. How could you possibly not feel sorry for her right now? All you have done is treat her with so much disdain and hostility and frankly I am tired of waiting for you to come around and see things from her side!"

"I do see things from her side, and that's why I suggested we take her to the police, there's no real reason for her to keep staying here," Troy said allowing that to sink in before he continued.

"What if those people who kidnapped her start looking for her, you saw her that day didn't you? So, what if we get caught in the crossfire, huh... what then?"

"This is not some Hollywood movie, T. Usually I'm the one coming with all these crazy theories and the fact that you're the one coming up with them now, only proves my point. And to be honest the way you're so set on pushing her out of this house is beginning to look suspicious."

Blinking back his shock from how accurate Darren's suspicions were, Troy turned his head away from him in case his face showed his guilt, and then he saw Reina standing at the foot of the stairs watching them, they hadn't even heard her come in over their squabble. She was actually very beautiful, with her jet black hair and almost red lips making her look like some Italian sex goddess. All these only served to infuriate his anger the more, it was like he was attracted to her and he hated himself for it.

"Perfect, now she's eavesdropping on our conversations," Troy scoffed at her as he ran his hands through his already messy hair.

"I'm sorry I did not mean to eavesdrop, but don't want to cause any more trouble. I'll just get a few things and leave if that's what you want." She was already walking back up the stairs to get her things but Darren's voice halted her in her tracks.

"Reina! You're not going anywhere, Troy and I were just hashing a few things out. You don't have to go!"

"Maybe she has a point Darren, she has caused enough trouble as it is," Troy said.

"The only person I see causing trouble here is you, Troy, so unless you want to be the one leaving this house, I suggest you get used to her presence in this house, I don't even recognize who you are right now."

"Darren, are you really asking me to leave because of some girl...."

"Enough!" They both turned to Reina in shock as she screamed. She went down the stairs slowly stalking towards Troy.

"If Darren wants me to stay, then I am going to stay, I also suggest that you get on board with that idea. In about a month you won't even remember my name anymore so please don't ruin your beautiful marriage because of some *girl*," saying the last part in an exaggerated hand quote, she stalked back to her room trying to contain her anger with him. She had been in her room trying to stay out of their fight, trying to be the good girl and stay quiet.

But she just could not hold it anymore, he was being a jerk and it was finally time she stood up for herself, she had been bullied by men all her life and she had been taking it in silence not standing up to them, but that stops now, she would no longer be bullied anymore.

Staring at her retreating back in shock, Troy felt only shame at how he had been treating her, she was one of his kind, even though he did not know her real story, she was still family and he had been treating her like she was the enemy. He should have been the one helping her, supporting her and backing her up like Darren had been doing throughout this her ordeal. But he was the one making things even more painful for her. He was disgusted with himself.

"Troy?" Darren called delicately to his back which was still turned back to him, "Are you okay?" he had been standing there still as a statue for a while, in his own thoughts.

"She gave you something to think about, didn't she?" Darren asked.

"I've been a fool." Turning back to Darren, he settled down in a heap into one of the stools by the kitchen island table and covered his face with his hands.

"That you have been," Darren said with some humor in his voice now that he saw that Troy was having a change of heart.

"I should go apologize to her."

"That you should."

"I can't believe how I've treated her all these weeks, she just needed a place to stay and all I've done is make this house hell for her."

"Well I can't believe I am saying this but, in your defense you were only trying to protect my family."

"Why are you even defending me right now, I've been awful," he said giving a dry a laugh.

Darren came around the kitchen table and took Troy's face in his hands kissing him softly on the lips.

"Go apologize to her, you are a good man Troy, I can't blame you for trying to protect us."

She's my family, too, Troy thought to himself and he had not even defended her. His secret gnawed at his chest and almost told Darren at that moment but he could not bring himself to that. He couldn't take it if he started looking at him like some freak.

Nodding his head, he stood up and placing another kiss on Darren's lips he walked up to her room.

Reina sat on her bed, her face in her hands, why couldn't she just keep her mouth shut, she thought to herself. She should have just stayed in her room until they had finished their argument. Why did she have to go talk to him?

She was sure they were going to send her away now, and Darren, oh he was going to be so disappointed in her that she had spoken that way to his husband, after all he had done for her. She hadn't even looked at his face as she had walked out of there unsure of what she would see.

They'd had so much fun today. He bought her ice cream and frozen yogurt. They had bought so many clothes, she was sure she had never had those type of fancy clothes in her life and no one had taken her shopping before. When they had finished shopping, they had gone to all the tourist attraction sites in L.A, and he had also taken her to a spot Kendall Jenner was known to frequent just so they could catch a glimpse of her.

Even though she still had no idea who Kendall Jenner was but from the looks of it she was a very glamorous person. She had never enjoyed herself the way she did today and she had gone and ruined it all just because she couldn't control her anger. She stood up and went to start packing a few things, thinking about where she would go from here, she had no idea how she would get to Arizona from here, but she was going to try her best and do it. She had looked after herself all her life, she didn't need anybody.

As she was packing her things, planning to take only things she really needed since Darren had gotten her almost everything she owned. There was a knock on the door, walking to the door, thinking it was Darren, she opened it ready with an apology on her lips. She saw Troy standing on the other side of the door, his hands raised to knock on it again.

"Troy, I am so sorry. I don't know what came over me. I shouldn't have said anything about your marriage and I know that, it wasn't my place and…"

"Reina, Reina, it's me who should be apologizing. You did absolutely nothing wrong."

Reina could only stare at him in shock, thinking he was only pulling a prank on her.

"Can I come in please?" Pulling herself together, she opened the door wider allowing him to come in, and closing it after him.

He walked slowly to the window and then turned to face her, his eyes catching the small bag she had been packing.

"What are you doing?"

"I was just packing a few things, nothing expensive, just a few basic things I may need. The things Darren just bought for me are still in the bags and the tags are still on them so he can take them back and recover his money."

"You don't have to go anywhere, Reina. I have been a prick and I don't even recognize myself with the way I've treated you."

"It's okay, you were just protecting your family."

"But that's the thing, I think you're my family, Reina, and I've been pushing that thought out of my mind for weeks now but I can't anymore. I've been living a lie for years now and you were the truth, so I felt threatened, so I lashed out in fear and for that I am so sorry, please forgive me," Troy said, his face filled with so much emotion.

"I don't understand, what do you mean, you're my family. You don't even know me."

"I feel like I do. I've been seeing you in my dreams for a while now, though not your face but someone that looks like you, with the exact same tattoo you have on your shoulder." Troy explained coming close to her.

"I saw it you that night we found you and I was cold with fear, I thought my past had come back to haunt me."

"What about my tattoo, what makes it so exceptional?" Reina asked trying to understand what he was saying.

"Because I have the same tattoo on my shoulder Reina, I am a werewolf, just like you a crescent wolf to be exact and I'm guessing you're from New Orleans." Opening his shirt, he showed her the tattoo on his shoulder, Reina gasped stepping back.

"Oh my God, I suspected you were a wolf too. I smelt it on you but I had no idea you were a crescent wolf too like me."

They stared at each other in thought for a moment.

'What do we do now? I guess Darren doesn't know you're a wolf," Reina said, warily.

"He doesn't and I want to keep it that way, please," he begged.

"Your secret is safe with me, Troy."

"What are you doing outside New Orleans? I thought Alpha never allows his wolf to leave."

"I could ask you the same thing."

"Well I was sort of banished, not officially but more or less."

"Wow."

"What about you?"

"I think my story may be similar to yours, Troy."

"I doubt that," Troy said smiling at her. She smiled back and his gaze dropped to those red lips suddenly becoming aware of how close they were. He looked up almost immediately but her eyes had already followed his and she did the same, staring at his lips.

And then softly, she kissed him slowly, he kissed her back gingerly once, as his mouth moved over hers and then as if remembering himself he stopped immediately gently pushing her away and walking farther away from her.

"That was a mistake..." he pushed his hands into his hair ruffling at hard.

"I am so sorry, I shouldn't have done that," Reina said apologizing profusely with regret. But Troy only shook his head, and left the room immediately.

Reina came down the stairs to find Darren and Troy already seated at the table. Darren looked up and smiled at her, gesturing for her to join them.

"Your food's getting cold, Reina," he said to her

She immediately knew Troy had not told him about the kiss, she had no idea what to make of that, but she walked down and joined them noting that Troy was avoiding her eyes. This was going to be awkward.

"It's finally nice to see that you guys are friends now." Darren beamed as he served their dinner.

"I won't go so far to say that we're friends Darren, but we are definitely no longer enemies." Troy smirked at her as he spoke.

Reina had no idea if he was flirting or teasing her, so she only smiled Darren, now avoiding his gaze.

"Well, so long as there's peace, then I'm for whatever it is, though I would prefer friends though."

They all laughed and ate their food as Darren entertained them with jokes from YouTube.

That night in bed, Troy tossed and turned, thinking about the kiss he had shared with Reina, he couldn't stop thinking about it, he had to tell Darren about it. Seating up and turning on the light, he tapped Darren, who jolted awake murmuring,

"Aww, what is it?" he complained blocking his eyes from the light.

"Wake up, I need to tell you something." Hearing the in his voice, Darren sat up faster and turned to him.

"I don't know how else to say this so I'm just gonna come right out and say it and I am so so sorry, but... I kissed Reina." There was a slight catch in Darren's breath when he heard what Troy had just said.

"What do you mean you kissed Reina, was it a peck?" He asked Trying to be calm.

"No... I kissed her on the lips, but it didn't mean anything."

"If it didn't mean anything then why did you do it, Troy?" Darren asked raising his voice in anger.

"I don't know. It just happened."

"Things don't just happen, Troy, we make them happen." He paused for a while, then continued. "Did you like it?"

"It doesn't matter Darren..."

"It does to me, answer the question. Did you like it? Be honest."

Bringing his head down, Troy wanted to lie, but he just couldn't. "Yeah," his voice was barely a whisper.

"Right. I'm just going to sleep on the couch, I need to think."

"Darren, don't just walk away. We should talk about this." Troy pleaded.

"I need to think, Troy." Darren grabbed a pillow and blanket and stalked out of the room leaving Troy alone.

The next morning, Troy came down to find that Darren had gone to work, Reina was already awake and making pancakes in the kitchen.

"Good morning, I'm making pancakes," she said, her voice unusually cheery.

"I told Darren about the kiss," Troy said in reply as he put on his suit jacket, and adjusted his tie.

"Oh," she said, her cheery mood dying instantly.

"What did he say, I should leave," she said washing her hands and making to leave the room.

"No, don't worry about it. We will be fine, besides it didn't mean anything, right?" he asked as his eyes went to her lips.

"Of course not."

"Then there's nothing to worry about. We'll talk about it when we get back. Okay?" With that Troy left for his office.

*****

Two days after Troy had kissed Reina, Darren had still not come to terms with the fact that kissed her, he knew Troy was Bi and he was attracted to other girls but he thought that now they were together, he wouldn't be attracted to them anymore but he guessed that was just wishful thinking on his part, both Troy and Reina had apologized, and he had forgiven them but he couldn't get it out of his head. Something had been nagging at the back of his mind all day but he could not ignore it anymore.

He sat up on his bed and tapped Troy awake.

"I think we should have a threesome," he said in rush.

Troy who was still dozing, jolted awake when he heard this, the sleep fled from his eyes.

"What! What do you mean a threesome, Darren. Are you crazy?"

"I'm not, just hear me out. I know you're attracted to Reina, I've seen the way you look at her..." Troy made as if to interrupt him but Darren only stopped him with his hand and continued.

"You don't need to say anything Troy, I don't judge you and I know she's hot, I mean if I were Bi I would rather you did it in my presence than behind me. Of course we would have to ask her first and see what she says." Troy could only stare at him.

"Well, what do you think?"

"No," he said simply and went to sleep.

"What do you mean no? Come on, Troy, I know you want to..."

"You don't know what I fucking want, Darren." They both paused, then Darren continued.

"Think about it, it's a good idea and you know it, you just think you'd hurt my feelings but you won't, in fact I think I might even enjoy it. So you don't have to feel guilty." Troy sat up again and looked at him for a minute.

"Are you sure?"

"Yes," Darren replied.

"Okay then, let's have a threesome."

The next morning, Reina comes downstairs to find Troy and Darren sitting on the table and watching her, it looked like they had been watching her for a while.

"Is there a problem, you guys want me to go right?"

"Calm your horses, woman, no one's asking you to go anywhere." Troy replied dryly. Visibly having a relieved sigh, Reina goes to pour herself a cup of coffee.

"We wanted to ask you something, and you have a choice to refuse. It's just a suggestion."

"Okay, anything."

We wanted to know if you would want to have a threesome with us," Troy said in a rush.

"Troy! I thought we agreed I would say it."

"Yeah, well, you were taking too long."

Darren sighed and looked back at Reina. "You don't have to say anything yet, just think about it first then..."

"Yes."

"What?"

"Yes, I will have a threesome with you guys. I think it would be fun actually."

"Alright then it's settled, we're going back to have a threesome."

***

That night, Troy and Darren returned from work earlier than normally did. Reina had gotten herself ready, she had shaved everywhere capable of being shaved and was a bundle of nerves. She had no idea what she was thinking when she agreed to having a threesome with Troy and Darren. She hadn't even known them for long and here she was accepting to have sex with them. She'd prepared dinner so when they came back, they had all settled on the dining table and ate dinner in awkward silence, the threesome they had discussed that morning hanging in the air but no one was willing to bring it up.

When they finished with their food, Darren and Troy cleared the table and did the dishes while she was too nervous to do anything other sit on the kitchen counter and watch them. Her eyes trained on Troy's ass as she tried to quell the desire that was raging inside her. Without thinking she got down from the counter and walked to where they stood, her hands going to his front and wrapping around his zipper just above his cock.

Troy stilled but did nothing to discourage her and she went on and pulled his zipper, Darren had noticed their interaction by now and just stood aside watching them. Reina pulled his pants down as he turned, now ignoring the dishes he had been doing. Reina immediately went on her knees and took out his already hard and swollen cock from his boxer briefs as she gave it a slow lick from the top to its base like she was licking a lollipop.

She then took just his tip into her mouth sucking on it hard as she stared up into his eyes which were trained on her. His hands fisted her long hair and he yanked her head forcing her to take all of him deep into her throat. She gagged and withdrew her head and he repeated the same process groaning loudly as his cock reached the back of her throat.

Darren unable to hold himself any longer walked closer to them and kissed Troy deeply on his mouth, Reina turned to him behind her and took out his cock too sucking it just as deep as she had been doing with Troy, they both raised her up, getting rid of their clothes as fast as they could and rolling on a condom Darren had produced from his pocket.

She wrapped her legs around Troy while Darren stood behind her, and she was lowered down so her dripping pussy was now level with his cock and he slipped inside her while Darren slipped his cock inside her tight asshole making her moan out in pain and pleasure

"Oh, that feels so good," Reina moaned out as they both pounded into her holes making her moan with each push.

"Oh God, I'm so close..." Darren said hissing in pleasure,

"Oh yes, I'm coming."

"Come for me, baby," Troy whispered in her ears as she came hard, her eyes rolling back into her head from the intense pleasure she was feeling, they both came almost at the same time groaning out loud and kissing over her shoulder. Reina was spent, and she wobbled a little when Troy settled her down from his body. They disposed of the condom and carried her back upstairs to their bedroom. She guessed the night was just starting.

Chapter 6

"What do you mean they lost the girl?" Samoa asked Azul, his right hand man who had come to deliver the bad news that Ziro and his men had lost Reina again.

"Ziro and his men sir. The girl has disappeared and they have no idea where she is," he repeated.

"Yeah, I know what you said. Motherfuckers! Their ego caused them to refuse my help when I graciously offered to help transport the girl," Samoa said angrily, almost in a shout.

"Ziro is here, sir, probably to grovel and ask for more time," Azul told him.

"He's here?" Samoa asked.

"Yes sir."

"Well bring him in then." He said waving his hand dramatically in the air.

"Right away sir."

He left the room just as Samoa picked up his glass of vodka, cursing under his breath. He knew they were probably going to mess this up.

It was just a matter of time, that was why he had offered to send his men with them, but Ziro's pride had gotten in the way. He wanted to see how he would talk himself out of this one. There was a knock on the door which interrupted his thoughts, setting down his drink and adjusting himself on the seat, he shouted for the person at the door to come in.

Ziro and two other men, the same two who had accompanied him before came in through the door, the air of arrogance which he had around him in his first visit had disappeared because he had come to grovel, hat in hand. Samoa gestured for them to speak not saying anything but

95

waiting for them to make the first pitch before the he said something.

"As I'm sure you must have heard Samoa, we've lost the girl. But my men are scrounging the woods and the streets as we speak, we will find her before the end of the week, just give us some time. We will definitely find her before the end of the week, besides she has no one here, no friends, no family, nobody. So she can't possibly hide for long." Ziro said all of this in one breath, trying to look remorseful, since Ziro had already paid them the agreed money.

When he finished explaining himself, Samoa simply watched them without a single expression on his face, he watched them until they were sweating almost fidgeting on their seats.

"You must have mistaken me for some kind of cunt Ziro, my money is in your account but your merchandise is not in my possession and you come into my place of business to show your face.

"There's no need to get all dramatic now, Samoa. We will bring your merchandise before the end of the day any moment from now my men will call me with good news."

"Now you are calling me dramatic," Samoa said dryly. "You are fucking calling me dramatic?"

"You know what I mean, Samoa."

"No actually, I don't." Samoa said seriously, sitting up from his laid back position before he continued. "All I hear is that I'm being cheated, and you're telling me to sit back and relax about it. Look here Ziro, you are simply a fool if you think you will cheat me and get away with it, find this girl still in the woods or the streets, she eluded you in London for almost five months, and London isn't even half as big as big as the united states, you may underestimate how efficient she can be, but I will not make that same mistake, my men will be joining forces with yours. We are going to come all the cities, neighborhoods and homes if you have to.

I will call my guys in L.A and San Diego to keep my eyes on her, I'm going to need a clear picture of the girl if you have one, let's just hope she hasn't left the west coast or worse the United States. Ziro could only nod his head in acquiescence, his mind had not gone to all these scenarios but he knew Samoa had a good point, even though it hurt him even to admit it to himself.

"Good, you and your men can see yourselves out, we have a lot of work to do. I will contact you with any update and I suggest you do the same. I don't want to be out of the loop Ziro, so inform me of any minor detail, you and your men may come up with."

Ziro and his partners stood up to leave, but Samoa was not yet done handing them their asses. "And... Ziro, I don't have to tell you this, but you're leaving the states until we find the girl and perform the sacrifice."

With another nod, Ziro walked out of the office.

***

Reina woke up on an unfamiliar bed, as she felt two warm bodies on her both side of the bed. The event from last night came to her in a hot flash and she smiled at the delicious ache she was feeling in her lower body, last night had been surreal. When Darren and Troy had asked her about them having a threesome, she went blank for five seconds and the next thing she knew, she was saying yes.

Of course she was attracted to Troy as she was the one who kissed him, but not in her wildest dreams thought about having sex with two guys. Feeling one of the guys stirring beside her, she froze unsure of whether it was going to be awkward or not, but Darren simply got up from the bed and walked buck naked into the bathroom, muttering a good morning in her direction.

Troy was still passed out so she gingerly got up from the bed in order not to wake him up and picked up her clothes from where they had discarded it last night, she attempted to sneak out of the room when Darren stuck his head out of the bathroom, tooth brush in his mouth.

"What do you think you're doing?" he asked.

"Ummm... going back to my room. Why? Is there a problem?"

"Oh, of course not. I was just wondering. Things don't have to be awkward. You know that, right? You can sleep here now, that is of course if you want to, not like anyone's forcing you to do that." He was stuttering out the words.

"Darren, just let the poor girl go back to her room in peace." Troy spoke from where he lay, his head buried in the pillows. They had no idea he was awake.

"Oh you're awake... Good morning, babe," Darren said.

"I'm just going to get started on making coffee," Reina said dashing out of the room, her face red as strawberry as blushed furiously.

Troy sat up and gave Darren a pointed look. "What? I was just trying to make her feel comfortable," Darren shrugged.

"By telling her, she could sleep here?" Troy said smiling at him affectionately.

"I just don't want things to be awkward, we don't know how long she is going to be here for and it would be weird if we are having sex and she is going to be sleeping in a different room." Troy didn't like the sound of Reina leaving, even though they had only been 'friends' for a short while, he could already feel himself getting attached to her even though he tried to fight the feeling, he couldn't help it.

"Let's just take things one day at a time, D. Baby steps, no need to over think anything, ok?

"You're right, no over thinking. That's a good idea," he said nodding.

"Of course it is." Troy smirked at him getting up from the bed and joining him in the bathroom, so they get ready for work.

It was movie night. Troy, Darren and Reina had just finished having dinner and they sat huddled together in the living room as Reina picked the movie they were about to watch. It was pouring heavily outside and the room was very cold so they were covered in blankets as they sat on the couch.

"I don't know which movie to pick, I have no idea which one's going to be good or not." Reina complained in front of the television.

"You can't go wrong, Reina. They're all good. You just have to pick one." They had been deliberating on the movie to watch now for almost twenty minutes. Reina, they were beginning to note was very indecisive and it took her ages to make up her mind about anything. Except of course the idea of the threesome, she has decided on that pretty quickly. The three of them had gotten a bit more comfortable with each other since the first time they had sex almost a week ago.

Although they had not done it again since to when Reina finally decided on a movie, she came and sat in the middle of the guys and when they saw the movie she had selected, they both groaned loudly.

"I thought you said I couldn't go wrong and they were all good," she pouted.

"They are, but did you really have to pick fifty shades of grey?" Darren mumbled, a trace of humor in his voice.

"What's wrong with fifty shades of grey? The title intrigued me," she said genuinely confused.

"Have you never really seen the fifty shades series?" Darren asked her.

"How the hell did that shit get into this house in the first place Darren?" Troy asked as he had heard it enough times Jane, his assistant to know the full gist of the movie much to his dismay.

"Well I wanted to spice up our sex life, so I watched it. Only for research purposes," Darren said and they all laughed.

"I had no idea our sex life needed to be spiced," Troy said in amusement.

"Oh now I'm really curious about this movie, we're definitely going to see it," Reina said shushing them as she played the movie.

They watched the movie in silence for about thirty minutes, and then things began to get really spicy when the first erotic scene came up, the scene of the elevator where Christian had Anna's hands up and kissed the daylights out of her had them all breathing hard. Before long, Troy's hand began to wander down Reina's legs up into her thighs, she only adjusted her legs to give him more room, enjoying the attention. By the first sex scene of the movie, the movie was all but forgotten as the three of them went at each other, kissing and touching and then Troy's shirt came off, Darren's shirt following as well.

"I think we should take this upstairs," Troy said as he was kissing Darren while his hand still remained between Reina's legs. Giggling softly, Reina nodded and they trailed upstairs stealing kisses and touches.

When they got to the bedroom, they slowly peeled off the remaining clothes they had on. There was an air of seriousness in the room, the playfulness was all gone as things became intense.

"Get on the bed," Troy told Reina, who obeyed quickly getting on the bed and facing the both of them, as they kissed each other, Darren had his hand around Troy's cock as they kissed with a sense of familiarity, like they had done it a thousand times which they obviously had. It was beautiful to watch, and then as if mentally communicating, they both turned to face her on the bed.

They both joined her on the bed, on either sides of her, Darren's hand wrapped around her nipples as he kissed her while Troy slowly moved her body until he was between her thighs, he gave her clit a soft kiss and Reina moaned out at the touch, he was teasing her and she enjoying it. Her hands went to wrap around Darren's length as she gave him a hand job, her hands forming a rhythm up and down his cock, Darren moaned into her mouth as the kiss became deeper, their tongues dueling with each other.

Troy slipped one finger into her pussy and her waist came off the bed from the shock, he held her down with his other hand as he slipped a second finger inside her, causing her to moan out and lose the rhythm she had on Darren's cock.

"Do you like that baby?" Troy asked as she sucked on her clit while simultaneously fucking her with his fingers.

"Yes... oh! Yes... please don't stop," and when his fingers coiled inside her finding that perfect spot, she came so hard, her eyes rolled to the back of her head. "Oh my God! Oh my freaking God yes!" she screamed as she came down, her hands useless as she abandoned Darren's cock.

When she opened her eyes, they were both watching her, and she felt the blush creeping on her cheeks.

"That was amazing."

Troy smirked wiping her moisture from his lips as crept up her body to kiss her, she tasted herself on his lips. Then he kissed Darren too, Reina sat up and took Darren's cook into her mouth loving the velvety feel of it. She licked him from base to the tip once and then again before taking him deep into her throat, he moaned out, his hands gripping her hair to hold her in place as she sucked him, she felt Troy position her hips and then slid his cock into her pussy from behind, she closed her eyes and moaned in pleasure, as they found a perfect rhythm, her sucking Darren's cock and Troy fucking her from behind.

Before long, they were all moaning loudly as their sex noises filled the room, the slap of flesh and the slurping noise of Reina sucking Darren's cock. When they came, they came together, collapsing in a heap of tangled limbs and sweaty bodies. "Oh my God, that was something." Darren said and they laughed.

"It sure was." And they fell asleep together, again.

***

Another full moon was coming, Troy thought to himself as he got down his car and walked into the house, he had just returned from a stressful day at work and he had not yet made any plans with Reina as to how they would transform, it was yet another month of lying to Darren and

102

although it pained him, he was kind of happy he had someone to share his burden with.

As he unlocked the door and walked in, the heard the noise of pots and smiled thinking Darren was already back and making dinner, but he was surprised to see Reina in an apron, as she made ruckus in the kitchen. She had not yet seen him walk in as she had on a headphone which Darren had gotten her to keep her company, she rarely went out except in the evenings to go on walks, so they got her some things to keep her busy while she was alone in the house.

He stood by the kitchen entrance and watched her as she swayed her hips to the music only her ears heard. Stopping suddenly as is sensing she was being watched, she took a knife and with the speed he had no idea she possessed, she threw the knife at him but he ducked just In time for the knife to miss and hit the wall exactly where he had been standing.

"What the fuck Reina!" He barked in shock still crouched on the floor.

"Troy... Oh my god... Troy." She gasped, taking the headphones from her ear and walking towards him. "I could have killed you, why would you sneak up on me like that?"

"I wasn't sneaking up on you, I was just about to announce myself before you almost maimed me to death," he said as they both stood straight to stare at where the knife was still lodged in the wall.

Removing the knife from the wall with a little force, Troy simply shook his head and walked past her, farther into the kitchen and depositing the knife back in its rightful position.

"Who knew I was living with a fully trained assassin who specializes in killing people with kitchen knives." Reina laughed at his joke following him into the kitchen to check what she was cooking.

"I swear I don't know where that came from. It was just a reflex action, I lost track of time and I had no idea you would be home by now. I didn't even hear you come in." Troy took a spoon to have a taste of what she was cooking as he listened to her but she pushed him away jokingly not wanting him to taste it before it was done.

"Who were you expecting anyway, you do know you're going to have to tell us who kidnapped you sooner rather than later right?" Troy asked sitting on the counter stool.

Reina gave him a look. "I choose later." She smiled trying to look cute and simply nodded in reply.

"Where is Darren anyway, is he home yet?" Troy asked.

"No, he's not, he probably won't be back until later." Reina answered.

Looking around as if he was going to tell a secret he said; "Good, I think we should talk about the coming full moon, you know, how we are going to transform and all that. It's not like we can do it here with Darren in the house."

Reina looked at him, flummoxed. She had not given it much thought. She didn't have to because she could control her transformation given the fact that she was a white wolf, but she had forgotten Troy was not blessed with that ability and he had to turn. She had not told him she was a white wolf and she had no idea how she would tell him now. He would probably find out if she did follow him out to transform but she wasn't about to tell him now, she did not know how he would react and she wasn't about to find out.

"What do you have planned, how did you do it before?" she asked, trying to keep her thoughts from her expression.

"Well I have a spot out in the woods, we can go there and no one would be around to see, just run around for a bit. Sometimes when I'm feeling primal, I kill a rabbit or two and then enjoy the freedom before changing back and returning home. Sometimes I hear the howling of the pack here in L.A but I never joined them."

"Why not? I've never transformed with a pack before," Reina said remembering how her first transformation went with her pack, they had discovered she was a white wolf immediately and everybody treated her differently, before the next full moon her parents had sold her out and she did like to think about her past so she came back to the present.

"They are not my pack Reina, if I transformed and joined them, they may see me as a threat or enemy and may attack." He explained gently to her.

"Oh! Yeah right." Even when she was with Ziro, she had never joined his pack to transform, she always had to hide so she would not be seen. Ziro had told her it was for her protection and safety but she now that it was all so he could keep her for himself.

"Although, the L.A pack are known to be the most peaceful werewolf faction. They are more hipster than traditional, so they may or may not attack but I'm not going to risk that." Troy explained further.

"I've never heard that." Reina said curious about the hipster werewolves.

"Well I'm just going to go up and get changed, the full moon is in two days' time, we leave at 11:30, just before midnight, okay? Make sure to be ready, in case we don't have the opportunity again before then." Reina knew it was because of Darren they may never be alone just the two of them before the full moon so she simply nodded and continued her cooking while he walked out of the kitchen.

***

Samoa sat in his chair on the phone talking to one of his contractors about one of his buildings which he was renovating into a five star hotel and Gambling arcade when there was a knock at the door. Azul, his right hand man opened the door and his head peeked in, Samoa waved him in, still on the phone.

"Fucking glass panes if that is what you need to complete the goddamn building Ben, I need the building to make me more money and not cost me more loses than I've experienced in years!" Samoa barked into the phone while he glared at Azul as if to ask him why the fuck he was disturbing his afternoon.

Azul mouthed a few words he couldn't make out, it looked like it was urgent so Samoa hung up the phone and asked, "Spit it out, Azul, What is it?"

"The girl, she has been sighted," Azul said not hiding the glee in his tone.

"That's fucking good news, what took you so long to say something." Azul looked up at him and then the phone, as if to point out it was because of him, Samoa.

"Well, she's been sighted in California, L.A to be precise. They say she's living with two guys and they are taking care of her." Azul explained.

"Wow! I did not see that one coming, I'm sure she found creative ways to pay her rent." Samoa said suggestively. Azul only laughed at that, not really knowing what to say.

"Do we know if any of them are like us?"

"The two guys are married actually but one is like us while the other one is human, we have no idea if they are connected or she knew them before but one of my guys did some digging on him, his name's Troy Dalton and he's got some shady past but get this, he is from the same pack as the girl.

"Hmmmm... and the plot thickens." Samoa quipped but Azul continued.

"His partner on the other hand is a doctor at the UCLA teaching hospital and they've been together for almost five years, no idea if he knows about us or not," Azul said as Samoa shakes his head as if disgusted by that piece of information.

"Place two of our guys on the doctor and another two on the werewolf, I want to know the minute she leaves the house and the next opportunity they have, I want captured alive without drawing any attention to us."

"Yes sir, and what about the other two?" Azul asked.

"What about them, Azul?" Samoa asked looking up at him.

"What should we do about them? What if they know about the girl, don't we have to take them out?" Azul asked again.

"No, it would draw more attention, attention we don't need. Just get the girl and get out, if they get in the way then take them out." Samoa said, dismissing him with the wave of his hand. "Get on it now."

"Oh! And tell Ziro and his men, they should join the search. After all, they were the ones who lost the girl in the first place." Azul nods and walks out of the office in haste, he was already on the phone making all the necessary calls.

***

Two days after Troy and Reina had discussed their plans for the full moon, the day had finally arrived, they sat in the room, the three of them, each of them engrossed in what they were doing, Troy was on his laptop, working as usual, Darren on the other hand was reading a medical book on the procedure he had to do tomorrow in the office, he usually did this when he had a very important surgery and he read up on it to know about anything that could go wrong.

In the OR and how he could fix it. Reina was on the floor, spread out and reading one of the books from her kindle, which Darren had gotten her. The room was comfortably silent and then, Darren yawned loudly breaking the silence and getting up.

"I'm beat, I need to go rest up. Important day coming up tomorrow," he said as he trudged slowly to Troy's side giving him a kiss on his forehead and then Reina's too before he went up. Troy and Reina stared at one another for a while waiting until they heard the door open and close before the Troy announced.

"I'm going to go get changed, make sure to wear something black so that we can blend with the night."

Reina stood up from where she was still sprawled out and nodded still a bit queasy from the realization that he was about to find out that she was the white wolf. Troy saw that she looked a bit sick and her face was pasty and thinking she was just nervous about the night transformation, he patted her in the back, trying to calm her nerves.

"No need to be nervous, Reina. I've done this for years now and no one ever comes to the spot where I transform. It's pretty deep in the woods and secluded, apart from animals we're going to be pretty much alone," he said in a calm voice, Reina only nodded.

"I know. I guess it's just a bit of nerves," she said.

"Nothing to be nervous about." He smiled at her and she smiled back, he kissed her softly on her lips making her heart skip a bit, she always reacted this way with him, but there was this connection she had with Troy that wasn't, there with Darren. She just could not explain.

"Go on. Meet me back down here in thirty minutes okay."

"Okay," she replied. They both went their separate rooms to change.

Taking the car, Troy and Reina back out of their garage into the street and drove out to the spot where they would transform, Troy had seen a car Packed by the side of the road while he was leaving but nobody was inside, he had been sure he saw somebody sitting there and staring at the house while he was in the bedroom and he'd looked out but he could not be sure.

He'd had the feeling that he was being watched for a few days now but he never saw anybody behind him, he had told Darren about it but he had just laughed it off and said Troy was just being paranoid because of Reina again. He did not even bother telling Reina because he did not want to spook her but the feeling had only intensified with the passing days and worse, he felt he was being watched by a werewolf.

They had to be more careful now and he would tell Reina to always make sure the door was locked whenever she was home alone, he doubted a locked door would stop a werewolf from breaking into the house but they could only hope, it was not as if they could sprinkle wolfs bane at the entrance without it affecting them or Darren asking about it. They just had to make do and hope that Reina's kidnappers, whoever they were never found them.

They drove in silence, the both of them in their own thoughts and then Troy parked the car at the entrance end of the city, where the city lights were afar distance and the houses around them were few and far between. Getting out the car and locking it, Troy took Reina's hand and led her into the forest, they both walked on in silence with only the noises of the night owls for company and an occasional howling in the distance.

By the time they came to a clearing, which Troy had made earlier, the moon was already at its peak and both their eyes were glowing in the dark like two orbs of light.

"This is the spot?" Reina said looking around as the place only served to remind her of the night she was being chased by Ziro and his men but she said nothing. Slowly they took off their clothes and stood naked, the moon bathing them in its radiance. Then the familiar sound of bone cracking and reshaping as they both began to transform under the moon.

Then Troy was fully transformed, when he turned to look at Reina, he was shocked to see a hauntingly beautiful white wolf staring at him.

"Reina?" he called her name like it was a question as they communicated through their minds, the white wolf simply nodded and suddenly it became clear to Troy, why she was on the run, why she was being kidnapped and why she was so afraid to leave the house for fear of being recaptured.

He had thought it was probably because her family was wealthy or something and they had kidnapped for ransom money. But now he knew that it was because of what she was. A white wolf, they had not seen one in a hundred years and they were as scarce as a unicorn.

"Why didn't you tell me?" he asked, coming closer to her.

"I was afraid I wouldn't be able to trust you," she answered.

"How could you even think that I and..." Whoosh! The sound of an arrow thrown missed his head almost an inch and lodged into the tree just beside where Reina stood. At first, Troy did not understand what had happened.

"They are here, we have to go, Troy!" Not to be told twice, they both ran as fast as they could, but the pursuers came after them just as fast. Some were wolves while the others were humans, as they were the ones throwing the arrows at them.

"Reina, who are these guys?" Troy asked as he ran alongside her.

"They are my past, Troy, and they've caught up with me. We need to get out of here," she said as one of the arrows hit her in her hind legs as they were running and she howled in pain, although she still continued running but in a slower pace.

One of the wolves was gaining on them and then he pounced on Reina, biting her hard but not hard enough as she tried to fight back but another arrow filled with wolfs bane had already made her severely weak. Troy pounced on the wolf still on Reina, biting deeply into his neck until he was bleeding so badly and then went limp on the floor. So they kept running through the woods and away from their pursuers.

Chapter 7

When they neared the road towards where their car was parked, they both transformed back and Troy carried Reina into the car, she was bleeding from her leg and shoulders from where the arrows had hit her, driving as fast as he could and running through all the red lights since it was already about two in the morning and the streets were empty.

Troy drove home looking back to check if he was being followed, but they weren't. Reina held her arms as she tried to stop the bleeding with a cloth. She had pulled out the two arrows before they got into the car. Before long, they arrived at the house and Troy drove roughly into the garage, he could not go to the hospital as that would only raise too much questions, so he came to Darren.

There was no way he could keep hiding all this from him anymore, he was going to have to come clean now. Although he dreaded it, he knew he had no other choice. Carrying Reina out of the car since she could not walk, he opened the front door and switched on the light, planning to keep her on the couch and go to call Darren but he was already sitting down on one of the couches, waiting for them.

The light jarred him up from where he had been dozing off and his eyes widened in shock, taking in their undressed state and all the blood. It was then Troy realized that he had not even put on his clothes.

"What the fuck, Troy!" Darren said in shock just as his medical instincts took over and he rushes to where Reina lay still, bleeding. She was already passed out and Troy was panicking thinking she was dead, Darren felt her pulse and nodded to Troy to help lift her up. They took her to the bathroom and placed her inside the bath tub.

"What the hell happened, Troy? Why is she bleeding out all over the place?" he asked as he worked without looking at Troy. He got out his first aid kit from their medical cabinet and poured a bit of methylated spirit on her wound and cleaned the wound to check how deep it was. Troy who was still in shock and simply stood there, still naked as he watched Darren work. He had no idea where to start his explanation from.

After checking the wounds to see that it wasn't as deep as he thought it was and it only needed stitches, Darren took his needle and thread and got to work on both her shoulders and legs.

After a while he was done stitching her up and was cleaning the wound with more gauze before wrapping it with a bandage, he cleaned her up with warm water after barking orders at Troy to go clean up in Reina's bathroom.

He dried her up before carrying her into the room and putting on one of his old shirts and boxers for her, her laid her on the bed covering her in blankets, he then stared at her for a minute wondering who she was and what kind of trouble she was in. He knew he should have been more worried about bringing a stranger into his home but he had been so moved to compassion.

Seeing her on the road like that, where they had found her and having just lost a patient. His guilt would have been soul-crushing if they had just left her there like Troy had suggested. He was still glad they brought her home, at least now he could say he'd had sex with a girl, but he couldn't still shake off the feeling that bringing her home might have been a big mistake, one he might regret sooner or later.

Darren was still deep in his thoughts when he glanced up and saw Troy walking in, now fully dressed. He simply stared at him allowing is face to show the question as he waited for Troy to explain what had happened.

"I have something to tell you."

"No shit," Darren said, dryly cutting him off.

Troy paused at that as if waiting for Darren to say something else and when he didn't, he continued, "You will have to promise not to freak out or anything, because what I'm about to tell you is pretty surreal and unbelievable but you have to promise to keep an open," Troy said waiting for Darren to reply.

"Does this have anything to do with why Reina is lying injured in our bed?"

"Yes," Troy replied him as he joined him on the other side of the bed. Darren promised, not really sure what to expect and Troy nodded, still not knowing where to begin, so decides to start from the very beginning.

"I'm a werewolf." He announced grimly looking into Darren's eyes as he spoke and letting him see how serious he was in his eyes. Darren stared back, his face blank like he had not fully registered what he just heard. Troy tried repeating himself making sure Darren heard him.

"I heard what you said the first time, Troy, I'm just processing what you are saying. What do you mean you're a werewolf? Are you kidding me right now? A girl almost died in our bed and this is what you tell me?" Darren said furiously getting up from the bed and walking to the other side of the room so as to not wake Reina.

"I will get to why Reina is injured but I wanted to start from the beginning so you would understand." Troy explained to him. "My family is originally from New Orleans and that is where Reina is from as well."

"What are you saying, Reina is one, too?" Darren asked not yet able to bring himself to say the word.

"Yes, that is exactly what I'm saying. We are from the same park and though I have never met her before until we picked her up on the road, I knew immediately that she was like me. There is usually a kind of connection among wolves from the same packs and when their kind is near, they can sense it." Troy paused again and seeing Darren watch him like he had horns and although he had expected it, it was still painful to see him look at him like he was a freak but he continued.

"We have the same tattoos on our shoulders and it's the tattoo of our faction, we are known as the crescent wolves." Troy showed Darren the tattoo like he had not seen it before and also Reina's which was on her good shoulder. Darren saw this but he still looked like he wasn't convinced so Troy continued still.

"I sneak out of the house on every full moon to transform and that's why you've never seen me in my wolf form and when we saw Reina that day on the road, I knew she was like so I panicked because I knew you would want us to look after her. I felt like my secret was going to come out any moment and I wasn't wrong."

"Is that why you were so against her staying with us?" Darren asked, his voice calmer than before, as if trying to figure out why Troy never talked about his past even when he tried to bring it up, why it always felt like he did not know him sometimes and other things he could not explain like how his eyes would sometimes glow in the dark, he usually attributed it to the lights or something but never in his wildest imagination would he have guessed he was married to a werewolf.

He had been married to one for almost five years and he had no idea about it. "Were you ever going to tell me?" Darren asked.

"I don't know, I always came so close to telling you but I'm a coward so I always chickened out. I love you too much and I was scared, I expected the worst. I thought you would probably leave me if you found out and you're the only good thing in my life Darren, I didn't want to throw it all away." Troy explained with so much emotion in his voice, his eyes were pleading with Darren as he explained as if begging him to understand.

"So then you never trusted me." Darren said disappointment clear in his voice.

"No, it wasn't like that, Darren. I did trust you."

"But not enough to tell me your biggest secret."

Troy had nothing to say to that. It wasn't that he did not trust Darren, he did, he was just too scared of what the outcome of his coming clean would do to their relationship, to their marriage. Darren simply nodded his head as if he had just come to a deep enlightenment and walked out the room but Troy followed him.

"Where are you going?" Troy asked behind him.

"I need space to take this all in, Troy. You can't just spring this on me and expect me to be okay," Darren said in a rush not even turning to look at him.

"I'm sorry, D. I'm sorry I never told you and if you need space. I'll give it to you but be careful. While Reina and I went into the woods to transform, some men came out and started shooting at us, I'm not sure who they are but I'm guessing they're the ones who kidnapped her. I don't think they followed us here but they knew we were coming so just be careful babe." Darren turned back to him and nodded before he walked out taking his car keys with him.

Troy sat there for a while, just staring into space and trying to come to terms with what had just happened. He felt like a massive weight had been lifted off him but he also felt like another kind of weight had just settled on him. He glanced at Reina on the bed, she was still as a statue and if not for the slight rise and fall of her chest to indicate she was still breathing, she looked deathly pale.

What had she brought on them? He thought to himself. All his life here in California, he had tried as much as he could to avoid anything that had to do with wolf drama. He stayed away from the L.A pack so he was never on their radar, he tried so much to stay out of trouble and now he was in trouble with a capital letter living under his roof. He was still trying to come to terms with the fact that she was the white wolf. He has always heard the tales about them but he thought they were a myth; having the freedom to turn whenever they wanted and not being controlled by the full moon.

It was no wonder she was on the run, he was sure a lot of people wanted her dead and now she was here, they were all at risk. Even his Darren.

As he sat thinking about his next course of action, an idea suddenly came to him, he was going to pay a few visits. They needed all the help they could get and if Reina was going to come out this alive, he was going to make a few allies. He could not leave her alone in this house though, someone was going to have to be here with her at the time since the men with arrow knew where to look for her.

He was sure they also knew their house. So he covered the whole entrance of the house with the wolf's bane he had hidden in the attic now that the cat was out of the bag, there was nothing to hide from Darren anymore. After he did that, he called his assistant Jane to cancel all his meetings for the next few days because he wasn't going to be available, he also called his partner Drew to cover for him with the executives, his excuse being that he was dealing with family crisis because Reina was his family and he would do anything to protect her and Darren. Lastly, he called Darren to find out where he was but it went straight to voicemail.

"Fuuuuuuuccckkk!!" he shouted. But he kept trying, when his third trial still went to voicemail, he left a message. Darren please pick up, I need to know you are safe and I need you to please come back to the house now, it's not safe out there.... Just text me when you get this please.

He completed the message and hung up. About ten minutes after he sent the message, Darren replied with a text telling him he was on his way home. Heaving a sigh of relief, Troy walked around the house locking all the windows and doors.

***

Ziro's anger level was at an all-time high, he was being treated like dirt by some barbarian Native American, all because of Reina. Forget the bloody sacrifice, he was going to kill her with his bare hands the next time he saw her and then he was going to kill Samoa as well for having the guts to speak to him like some lowlife lackey and not the alpha that he was, all because he had more money.

He had lost three good men now, all because of Reina, he had not even informed their families yet. He had piling up excuses and excuses hoping he could sell them for a good price and then settle these families so that they would be quiet about it.

His position as Alpha in England was being threatened enough as it is and any more mishaps could get him impeached. He had thought the trade-off was going to be simple until that bitch had managed to slip through his fingers again. She was going to pay for all the trouble he'd gone through for sure. Sitting in his car as his driver drove him to Samoa's place. He was thinking of all he'd lost, his pride, his men and now if he wasn't careful, he could lose his money *and* his Alpha title. No way that was happening.

He had been summoned again by Samoa, the audacity of that man. But he had to play the obedient fool for a little while longer, he just had to let go of his anger for a little while, after the full moon capture had gone south. His men were now watching the house but Samoa had told them not to attach so as to not draw much attention to themselves.

His thoughts were to "fuck that" and capture the girl while they could before they realized they were being watched and ran away again. But he could not do that.

"Fucking barbarians," he muttered to himself.

"Yes sir!" his driver called out to him, thinking he was addressing him. Waving him off, Ziro went back to his thoughts while looking out the window. About seven minutes later, they arrived at one of Samoa's clubs which was his main office. The club was a very big building and he could feel the jealousy in his veins that Samoa got to control all this while he had almost nothing back in England.

Walking into the building with his driver following him closely behind, he took the way that led to Samoa's office now conversant with the club having being there more than once.

Samoa sat in his chair in his office as he spoke with one of this men, whom Ziro recognized from his first visit as the man who introduced him, they both stopped talking when they saw him and this made him suspect something although he did not call them out on it. Samoa motioned for him to seat down not seeming to mind that he had just barged into the office without even knocking.

He had done it intentionally to get a rise out of Samoa, to give him an excuse to lay into him but Ziro did not get the reaction he had expected. He sat down without saying a word and then Samoa began.

"We called you here to discuss strategy," Samoa said looking at them both on a dramatic pause before he continued, "This is the second time the girl has slipped through our fingers and it seems we have underestimated her abilities as the white wolf. A mistake I don't plan on making." He gave his assistant a look which Ziro did not understand but his assistant did.

"We have them under watch now, for the next 48 hours and our plan is to grab the girl without making a fuss as much as we can.

Ziro smiled and shook his head at this causing Azul to stop what he was saying so they both turned to him. "Do you have a better idea?" Samoa asked him, the anger evident in his voice.

"Of course you wouldn't want to raise a fuss Samoa, you have not lost anybody. I've lost three men, three fucking men and you're preaching to me about raising a fuss. I want the head of the man that was with her on a dish. I want to go take them out so they know not to mess with me," Ziro said, his voice rising in anger. "I don't expect you to understand Samoa, you lost none of your men that night."

"I don't know how things are done back in England but here in America, we have accountability and so three men dying mysteriously in their home especially in a city like Los Angeles is going to raise too many eyebrows, attention like that is what we don't need. So unless you want to keep losing more men, I suggest you do as I say, no questions asked. Am I clear?" Samoa said to him in a stern voice as Ziro nodded, trembling with the effort he took to swallow his anger and not storm out of the office.

"Good, now I see that your emotions are a bit high from last night so why don't you go back home and bury your dead. We will meet tomorrow again, same time. We plan on attacking in two days, the girl is injured so the time to strike is now." Ziro stood up almost immediately not bothering with any form of pleasantries and he stormed out of the office, motioning to his driver to follow him as he left the club.

***

The car noise jolted Troy from where he had been dosing in the sitting room, startled, he jumped up and grabbed the baseball bat he had been holding but had fallen off while he was sleeping, he walked to the window to check who it was that and was relieved to see that it was Darren coming in, glancing at the time, he saw it was a few minutes past midday.

He had been dosing for almost an hour. Keeping the bat aside, he rushed to the door and opened it just as Darren was about to open it, motioning him to come in quick, Troy locked the door as fast as he could, leaving Darren to be shocked at his strange behavior.

"What is going on, Troy, I got your message." Darren asked walking inside as Troy followed behind him still staring out the window.

"That vehicle," Troy said pointing walking towards the window and pointed as Darren came up behind him. "That vehicle's been out there all morning. It was there when Reina and I were going to transform and even though it wasn't there when we got back, it's been there ever since you left."

Darren felt a chill in his bones.

"Who are these guys and why do they want her so bad? Are they scientists who know what she is? Is that why they want her so badly?" Darren asked filled with confusion but Troy shook his head as they walked away from the window trying not to raise any suspicions and went up the stairs to where Reina was still passed out.

Troy did not realize the arrows were laced with werewolf's bane but he was sure because that could only explain why Reina's wound was taking so much time to heal. They both sat on the bed and stared at her.

"We should talk about this T, now am not saying I forgive you for keeping such a big secret from me all these years, but I guess understand. I've been thinking about it and I can't imagine how it must have felt for you carrying this around you all these years and not having anyone to share it with. I wish you had told me though even If I understand, I'm still mad you did not trust me enough but you trusted her and I get it since she's just like you too." Darren said, looking at Reina as he spoke. Troy was quiet for a long time as he thought of what to say to him.

"I'm so sorry, baby. I don't know why I couldn't trust you but I see now that I should have and I just hope I haven't ruined..." His voice broke a little as he tried to control his emotions. "I love you Darren, more than I ever thought I was capable and I'm so sorry for not trusting you, you don't know how sorry I am but I hope you see it in my eyes."

Darren wiped the tears rolling down his cheek.

"I do, I forgive you," Darren said to him. "How could I not forgive you."

They both stood up immediately and ran into each other's arms, kissing desperately like it would be their last. When they came up for air, Darren smiled at him. "So, I'm married to a real life werewolf. Hmmm, that is not something I ever thought I'd say in my life. They both laughed at that and kissed again ,this time even more deeper than the last. When they separated Troy's face became serious and he turned to Reina on the bed.

"We have to protect her. These people who are after her, they're not scientists like you guessed. They're werewolves like us too but not from the same pack." When he saw the confused look Darren gave him he paused to explain. "We wolves are divided into packs and they're scattered all around the world, your pack is like your family and they share the same bloodline, not like bloodlines in terms of consanguinity, but bloodlines in the sense that they were all turned by the same wolf, that is their ancestors were turned by the same wolf. That's how the packs are divided. Now Reina and I belong to the same pack from New Orleans and that is why we share a connection, a kind of bond I can sense when she's near that's why I was having dreams about her even before we met." Darren's eyes widened in realization.

"She's the one you've been dreaming about all these weeks?" he asked. "Yeah and I guess it's because she was in Nevada. I have not come across a New Orleans wolf in over 10 years since I left home and she's the first one I've been seeing that Darren was about to ask him about his family and why he left home, Troy continued in a rush not allowing him to ask.

"Reina is a special kind of werewolf and that's why these guys are after her," Troy said.

"You mean these dogs?" Daren said, twitching his brows at his joke.

"Don't ever make dog jokes to a werewolf, Darren," Troy deadpanned.

"Oh, I'm sorry, I have no idea how these things work," Darren
apologized, not wanting to hurt Troy's feelings.

"Although given the situation, we could call them dogs," Troy said jokingly and Daren elbowed him slightly as they laughed.

"Okay so Reina is a white wolf," Troy continued and Darren's eyes widened in amazement, although he had no idea what it meant but it sounded like she was really special. "Yeah she's a white wolf, the first one in over hundred years now and they have special abilities which other werewolves usually seek, so when one white wolf comes up, the other ones try to steal these abilities by performing a sacrifice on the white wolf to get those abilities for themselves, thereby killing the white wolf in the process." Troy explained.

"Wow that's so horrible, poor Reina, she must have been on the run her whole life." Darren said. "Did you know who she was?"

"No, I had no idea she was the white wolf until last night. She must have thought she couldn't trust me with it," Troy said.

"Oh yeah, and how does that feel," Darren said, giving him a look.

"Not good at all. So we need to protect her, Darren, with all we can."

"But how we can we fight off werewolves, last I checked, you're the only one with the powers here and I can't do anything at all," Darren said giving Troy a panicked look. "I know that's why I came up with a plan but I'm going to need you to be on guard duty, you'll have to call in sick at work or something. I'm going to go have a meeting with some people that I think will agree to help us. They are the L.A pack, I've never actually met them before so it's not like we're friends or anything like that, but from what I've heard they're really free people, and they are not power hungry wolves like some packs can be, so I'm going to go and ask for their help and see what they say," Troy said.

Darren gave it a thought for a minute then a thought struck his mind. "What if the same people who are looking for Reina are the LA pack?" Darren asked.

"It's not possible. One, I got kind of a good look at one of the wolves and I know for a fact that they are definitely not the L.A pack. Two, I know what pack they are probably not far to have followed her here I'm guessing it's Nevada since that's where we picked her up from but only Reina can tell us for a fact. We'll just have to wait until she wakes up!" Troy told him.

"Okay then, won't you need like protection or like a gun or something?" Darren asked him, afraid he was going to see a pack of wolves unarmed.

"They don't believe in guns, D. They're kind of hipsters, like hipsters wolves, they're vegan. They don't believe guns and all that so they're not going to harm me," Troy said to put his mind at ease,

"Alright then, just be careful babe, I'll hold forth down here." They kissed and Troy went out.

***

As he drove out of their drive way, Troy punched in the address of the last pack's alpha, into his G.P.S, his house was in Beverly hills one of the swanky neighborhoods there but he had never been to that area so he had no idea where he was going to. He had gotten his address from the only person who knew he was a wolf in this town before now. They had met one night about two years ago when he had gone to transform in the woods, he always tried to steer clear away from other wolves but Luca had wandered too far away from his pack and they had met. Troy had helped him get back to his pack on the promise that he would not tell another soul about him.

After that night they had kept in touch every once in a while and had even met up once in a while for beer at a bar. Troy had told him very little about himself but Luca had explained to him almost everything about the L.A pack and that was how he had known so much about them.

After he had called Jane and Drew earlier, Luca was the last person he called and he had gotten the address of the alpha from him, after explaining his situation to him, Luca had even offered to drive him there but he did not want to put his life at risk instead he'd simply asked Luca to meet him there so as to make the introductions and smooth the way for him. It would strange to just walk into the alpha's home and demand for help without any help. Luca was his in and he was just grateful he had a lifeline at this point.

After driving for an hour 30 minutes, he came to a big mansion and from his G.P.S, he had arrived at his location. He parked outside the gate not sure if he should drive in or not so he called Luca while admiring the neighborhood, it was probably filled with celebs and he smiled as he thought that Darren would have loved to come to this area, probably to see if the Kardashians lived there.

Luca picked up the first ring.

"Hey, where are you? I'm parked in front," Troy told him immediately cutting to the chase. "Yeah just drive in bro, I'm already at the house, he's expecting you," Troy sighed in relief and restarted the car driving in, the gates opened automatically as he drove in and closed the same way. His jaw slacked in awe as he took in the magnificent beauty of the expensive house. He drove through the long driveway and parked right in front of the house just as Luca came out to join him.

"Hey buddy, come on in. He's expecting you," Luca said as Troy got out of the car. He was short but he had a buff athletic build, his hair was sunburned a deep golden brown and he looked like your typical surfer dude.

Troy followed him as he led him into the large foyer, it was like walking into a palace, there was gold everywhere. Even massive head of a wolf hanging on the wall was in gold color, Troy could not help staring around him, they walked on and entered a large living room where a small man sat on a very big chair and there was a young woman at his side, massaging his toes as he reclined back in the chair with his eyes closed. He was wearing only a white singlet and boxer briefs.

Clearing his throat loudly as if to announce their presence, Luca gesture for Troy to come in as he realized he'd been standing at the entrance and taking it all in. The little man lifted his bald head to see who had interrupted him. Troy's only thought was how this tiny man could be an alpha.

"You are wondering why I'm so little and still the alpha right?" The man asked Troy as if reading his thoughts. How the hell was that even possible. Troy thought to himself but he quickly schooled his face in case whatever he was thinking next showed in his expressions.

"Of course not." Troy denied even though he was sure the man did not believe him.

"Pinzu, this is Troy, Troy Dalton. He's the one I told you about, the person that saved my life. I owe him everything and he's been a very good friend to me." Luca glanced at Troy as if compelling him to play along because Troy did not remember ever saving his life but he continued.

"He's facing some problems with his personal life and he has come to seek our help."

Motioning for the girl at his feet to leave, Pinzu ordered them to seat down before he spoke. "I'm sure the man can speak for himself, Luca, or can't you, Mr. Dalton?" Pinzu asked looking over to where Troy sat with a questioning gaze.

"I can, Mr. Pinzu."

"Just Pinzu is fine." Pinzu interrupted.

"Pinzu," Troy corrected and continued. "Like Luca said I'm Troy Dalton and I'm also a wolf, although not from your pack.

"How long have you lived in LA?" Pinzu asked him.

"Uhm... about eleven years now," Troy replied, not sure why he was asking.

"So, you have lived here for over a decade and have not made yourself known to us." Pinzu asked with a raised eyebrow.

"I did not want to cause any trouble." Troy answered as Pinzu simply stared at him motioning him to continue. "I have a wolf now, currently under my care, she's the white wolf and a lot of people want to get their hands on her because what she is. I'm coming to you to seek your protection, for not just her but also for myself and my husband."

"Why are you so sure I won't grab the white wolf for myself? After all, I'm also an alpha and I will need her for my pack."

"I have it on good authority that you are a good man Pinzu, and you wouldn't kill an innocent woman just to make your pack stronger." Troy said, hoping with all his heart that Luca was right and Pinzu was the good man he said he was. Pinzu thought about it for a while with his head bent, and then as if coming to a decision, he raised his head; "I'll have to meet this girl." Troy was about to argue, telling him Reina was sick at the moment but Pinzu stopped him with a finger.

"If I'm going to sacrifice my men for this woman then I want to meet her and I want to know for a fact that she is indeed who you claim she is," Pinzu said.

"You want her to transform in front of you?" Troy asked.

"Yes, we all know the myth of the white wolf. So if she can't transform without the full moon, I'll kill you myself."

"Okay. Those are reasonable demands, although she can't come out today. She's been injured, we'll come tomorrow." Troy assured him.

"Good."

"Thank you so much, Pinzu, you don't know what this means to my family." Troy said standing up as Pinzu simply stood up. Luca joined him, saying their farewells as they left the beautiful mansion.

"What do you think?" Luca asked Troy.

"What can I say Luca, I hope he helps."

"He will, just hang in there." Luca replied as they both got into their car and went their separate ways.

Chapter 8

It was already dark by the time Troy drove into his own driveway, the vehicle that had been there earlier was nowhere to be seen. The street looked like it was deserted. He got out of his car, locked it and hurriedly walked into the house, worried that they had gotten to Darren and Reina.

"Darren! Reina! Darren!" The house was silent and he could feel his palpitating from fear until he heard Darren answer him as he came down the stairs. He could hear the resounding noise of his relief when he heard his voice.

"T, we're up here."

Troy walked as fast as his legs could carry him and enveloped Darren in a fierce hug.

"I thought they had taken you, the vehicle was no longer there so I thought they had already come to take you." Troy said with fear still in his voice, which he was trying to shake off, he was becoming paranoid and he hated it.

"It's okay. We're safe. How did the meeting go?" Darren asked as he walked upstairs to where Reina was still sleeping.

"It went better than I expected, although he is asking to see her tomorrow. Has she woken up yet?" Troy asked.

"No, not yet. But the wound healed, like it vanished from her arm like it was never there, but she still hasn't woken up," Darren explained.

Troy nodded, he had expected that she would heal fast, she was the white wolf after all. They walked into the room to find her still sleeping, color had returned to her face and she was no longer looking sick.

"She looks better than she did this morning." Troy noted.

"Yeah, her pulse is strong and she looks alright but I have no idea why she's not waking up," Darren said. They sat at the bed and watched her.

"Have you eaten at all today?" Darren asked, but Troy shook his head. Food was the last thing on his mind and he did not feel like eating.

"I haven't really had the time." His stomach grumbled almost immediately as and they smiled at each other.

"I'll go fix you a sandwich." Darren said.

"Thanks, babe."

Troy sat there staring at Reina as Darren left the room, he wondered why she has woken up yet, she looked like she was just sleeping and not passed out. He thought about his meeting with Pinzu, grateful now that they had someone on their side. He kept thinking back to when they had transformed and he realized she was a white wolf, the way she had looked at him as if he was going to attack. He didn't blame her though.

She had probably lived her whole life on the run. Darren came back into the room with a plate of sandwich and a glass of milk in the other hand. Laughing, Troy collected it with a grateful smile.

"I think I'm going to need something stronger than milk babe." He said. Darren did not even crack a smile.

"You're going to need your strength." They sat in silence for a while, Troy eating his sandwich while Darren watched.

"So tell me about the meeting." Darren told him the minute Troy finished eating.

"Well, like I told you before, the LA pack are usually free and kind, so I went to meet their Alpha, he looked a little weird but okay, I guess. I told him about Reina although now that I think about it he didn't look too surprise about Reina, or me." Troy said with a thoughtful look on his face but he continued "Yeah so I basically just summarized the whole story to him, he then asked to see Reina. He did not fully agree but I have a good feeling he's going to, he just needs to see for himself that she's real."

"I don't really like this Troy, you could be walking into a trap, what if he kills you and then they use Reina for the sacrifice." Darren asked.

"They won't babe, Luca gave me his word and I trust Luca." Troy replied him trying to get him not to worry.

"Okay then, if you say so, but you should still go with some form of protection, like a gun or something," Darren told him adamantly.

"I will if you want me to." As they were still talking about how best to guard the house, Reina made a sound like a whimper from the bed. They both turned to her when they heard and rushed to her side, she was already awake as she tried to get her bearings looking around her like she had no idea where she was; then her eyes rested on Darren and Troy who were watching her as if she was about to bolt.

"Hey guys." She said, her voice a little bit weak.

"Hey baby, how do you feel?" Darren asked as he felt her head to know if she was running temperature.

"I feel okay, a little bit groggy but okay." Then as if remembering the events of the night before, her hand flew to her shoulder, "I was shot?" she said like it was a question.

"Yeah, you were hit with an arrow, and I think the arrow was laced with wolfs bane but Darren got it out and treated the wound, it disappeared. I guess one of your abilities as the white wolf is that you heal fate than a normal wolf?" Troy asked her and she nodded in reply.

Glancing over at Darren, "Thank you Darren, I'm guessing now you know everything," she stated.

"Yeah, Troy got me up to speed on what you guys have been doing behind my back," He said, although there was no resentment in his voice. "We're really sorry about everything."

"I'm really sorry for bringing this kind of trouble to your doorstep, I'm just going to get a few things and skip town. I'm the one they want so if I disappear they will leave you both alone," Reina said getting up from the bed, but Troy and Darren held her back down.

"It's okay Reina, how long are you going to keep running, they won't rest until they find you and running around the world is not going to stop them," Troy said to her.

"So what do you suggest I do then, I can't take down two packs," Reina said almost in tears, "and I can't ask for your help in doing that, you've already done enough," she said. "

Why don't you tell us why they after you in the first place," Darren asked. Reina looked at both of them, at a loss of words.

Then she started, "My name is Reina Delores, I'm a New Orleans crescent wolf, just like you Troy, although now I can't say I'm even one of them, my parents were poor, and I don't mean small house, minimum wage poor. I mean trailer trash, south side poor, my mother was a drunk and the only time I ever saw her sober was when she would transform during the full moon. The pack always transformed together and one you were eighteen, you start to transform into a full werewolf. A month after my eighteenth birthday, when it was time for me to turn. I wasn't even going to college because there was no money for that and my grades were good enough to get a scholarship to any good colleges. So on my first night of transformation, we went bayou with the other werewolves to turn, I was so excited about that night, even my mother was happy for me, and she was a bitter woman so that is saying something.

"But before the moon was fully in the sky, I started changing, my bones cracking in the worst possible way, I had expected the transformation to hurt because of course we had always been told it was going to hurt but I did not expect the pain to be so bad. At first I didn't see any big deal that I was turning before everybody else, I thought it was probably because it was my first time.

"But I was not the only first timer there that night and when I fully changed and my fur was white as snow everyone was looking at me, I didn't even notice it until I looked at myself and I saw that I was white. And then every other person transformed, there was black, brown, brown and black, grey and so on but I was the only white wolf, and that was when I knew that something was wrong," Reina stopped talking for a while, her eyes glazed over as if she had been transported back as the past.

Darren went down to get her food to eat, even though she said she was not hungry. After she had finished eaten, she continued, "See, we'd always been told stories about the white wolf, but I always thought they were a myth. I mean a werewolf who was not controlled by the full moon? That was too good to be true. Until I became one myself, when I saw the way they were all looking at me, I ran without even thinking about where I was going to, I expected them to come after me but they didn't, not even my mother, she was looking at me like I was a freak.

"I transformed back into my human form and hid in the bayou, I was naked and cold and had nowhere else to go so I went back home, hoping my mother would at least act like my mother for once in her life but by the time I got, some men where in the house with my mother, before I could bolt again, they grabbed me. I pleaded with her to help me but she said I'd served my purpose as her daughter and she'd done her part, she was holding a duffel bag they'd given her, probably filled with the money she was paid to sell her daughter to be used as a ritual she was quiet again, and the room was so silent you could hear a pin drop.

"Oh, I'm sorry you had to go through that Reina," Darren said, ever the sympathetic one.

"Oh don't worry about it. I got over it quickly. I was sold to the alpha to be used as a ritual for the whole pack, my blood would break curse of the full moon and they would be able to change at will and not only during the full moon. They pumped me full of wolfsbane. And were about to begin the ritual but I somehow escaped, the details are a bit unclear but I found myself inside the bayou, naked and covered in blood. I thought it was my blood but it wasn't, it was after I left the bayou and stole some clothes from a nearby thrift store that I heard from somebody who hadn't known who I was that I had transformed during the sacrifice and killed seven other wolves. I couldn't believe it but I knew I couldn't go back home, I scrapped around Louisiana for about two years before I met Ziro. I had sensed he was a werewolf and I guess he sensed me too, I explained to him that I needed a job, any kind of work he had and he told me he lived in England.

"I already surmised he was British from his accent but I thought he lived in America, so when he offered to take me back to England. I was so relieved, I thought it was finally over, thought I was finally escaping from my past and having a new life, I thought I could start afresh in new country miles away from New Orleans.

"I went with him and he became my mentor, he treated me like I was his own daughter and his family welcomed me, even his pack. I never told him I was a white wolf though and I had no idea he knew. I stayed with him for almost two years and within that short period, he taught me so much, he taught me almost everything I know. He was the alpha of their but I never transformed with them, I always went somewhere else to change.

"Almost two years after I was Ziro and his family, I had this boyfriend and he knew everything about me including the fact that I was a white wolf. I thought we were in love but he had just being dating me on Ziro's orders to get whatever information he needed about what I could do as a white wolf.

"One night, Ziro and eleven other men who were the head of all the wolf families captured me, they are known as the 12 for the twelve families of the wolf pack and they were about to perform the blood ritual on me but I escaped again until you guys found me." Reina finished, it was almost midnight by the time but they kept listening to her without batting an eye. "So that's it, that's my story. Every single important detail." Troy and Darren stared at her, trying to process everything she had said.

"Guys, say something," she prompted them.

"Sorry, we are just trying to process all that," Darren replied her.

"I don't even know what to say, I'm so sorry for giving you a hard time when you first got here," Troy said but Reina waved him off.

"It's water under the bridge. Besides, you saved my life, so you've made up for your past transgressions," she said as she smiled at him.

"This Ziro sounds like a real asshole," Darren said and they all laughed.

"Trust me, he is," Reina said.

"Troy's come up with an idea of how we can stop them," Darren replied as they both turned to Troy to expatiate on that.

"I have a friend in the L.A pack and he kind of owed me a favor so I asked him for a meet with their alpha, he honored my request and I met with him yesterday. I explained our situation to him and asked for his protection and also help in fighting anymore future attacks and he hasn't totally agreed yet, but he wants to see you." Troy explained.

"See me? What if we are walking into a trap?"

"Exactly what I told him." Darren chimes in and got a look from Troy, telling him to shut the hell up.

"It's not going to be a trap, Luca is a good person and he wouldn't let me meet his alpha if he knew it was going to harm me. Besides, like I already told Darren, the LA pack don't believe in violence unless it's to protect a loved one. They are like hipsters." Troy explained to a still suspicious Reina.

"Alright then, if you trust them, I guess they must be good and it's like we have an alternative." Reina finally agreed.

"There's something else though," Troy said slowly gauging their reaction.

"What is it?"

"He wants you to transform before him so he can see for himself that you are indeed the white wolf," Troy said in a rush.

"Why the hell would he want to see me transform? Is it that necessary? Why would you lie about something like that?" Reina asked in quick successions.

"It's just for him to see that you are the white wolf, no harm will come to you while I'm there Reina, I promise," Troy said with a stern resolve making Reina nod in belief and satisfaction, she just needed to know she was safe and with Troy she's always safe.

The three of them came together in an intimate hug on the bed, "I need you both," Reina said, her tone not masking the need in her voice.

"I'm not sure that's advisable, Reina, you were just shot last night," Darren said trying to be the voice reason but failing when Troy wrapped his hand around his cock.

"No, I'm fine. I'm better than I've ever been," Reina murmured, dragging his face close to and covering his lips with hers, her hand going to Troy's cock in front of her while Darren was behind her on the bed. She alternated between kissing Darren behind her and twisting her neck to kiss Troy. They peeled off her clothes slowly as she raised her hands to help take them off faster. They also took off their clothes and came back to join her on the bed.

Troy bent his head and took her taut nipple into his mouth making her moan out in pleasure as Darren's fingers went to her clit and finding moist warmth, he began to rub her numb to a quick orgasm, she gasped loudly as the soft tremors made her weak with intoxicating pleasure.

"Tell me if I'm not doing it right," Darren whispered in her ear kissing her nape. "You are perfect, keep going.... I'm going to come... Uhhnnnn!" She screamed as she came all over Darren's fingers. As the tremors subsided, Troy lifted one of her thighs over his as he took his length in his hand and rubbed it over her already sensitive pussy making her shiver a little before entering slowly, making her gasp from the feeling of him expanding her tight walls with his cock.

Then she felt Darren behind her prodding her back entrance with his fingers before using his cock to impale her ass. "Uhhhnnnn," she screamed from the feeling of fullness. Her ass was burning but the pleasure of Troy massaging her clit while moving slowly inside her, distracting her from the pain. "Are you ok?" Darren asked pausing, his voice tight from the strain it took him to pause.

"Yeah, keep going," Reina replied and he didn't need any more encouragement. They began to move inside her in a see-saw motion, Troy pulling out and Darren pushing in, the pleasure was so intense that she came almost immediately.

Her walls tightening as she milked their cock inside her, triggering their orgasm as they followed behind her, both coming undone at the same time. They lay still, sweat dripping from their bodies as they tried to catch their breaths.

"That was amazing," Reina whispered against Darren's lips making him smile, then turning to kiss Troy as they both pulled out of her and laid together in a tangle of arms and limbs. They fall asleep within seconds of the other after making small talks about their past.

***

Samoa sat in his office with Azul and Ziro seated before him, he had just been told that the werewolf whom Reina had sought refuge had just been to the house of the L.A pack's alpha. He could already guess his reason for such visit and he was going crazy with anger, the involvement of the L.A pack complicated things a little for them but he would not let that deter him. The L.A pack are known for their free and liberal approach to life as a werewolf, they did not believe in violence but peace. So they could use that to their advantage.

"Sir, sir!" Azul called his attention to the meeting.

"I was saying we could grab the girl the minute she steps out of the house."

"What if Pinzu already has boys protecting them? Huh!" Samoa asked.

"Then we kill them all and just grab the just grab the girl since she's the only one we actually need," Ziro said.

"It's always about the killing to you, isn't it?" Samoa asked.

"Well it's more efficient, wouldn't you agree?" Ziro raised his eyebrows.

Ignoring him, Samoa turns to Azul. "Just monitor them for now and wait for my signal." Azul nods and leaves the room leaving just Ziro and Samoa in the room.

"I need to go back to my pack, Samoa. This is dragging on for too long. I have matters I need to go back to and handle." Ziro complained as he stood up from where he was sitting to pace the room.

"You forget that it was because of your fuckup we are in this situation to begin with. If you had not lost the girl that night, the ritual would have been done by now and I wouldn't be here either, so think about that the next time you want to raise your voice at me, Ziro."

Ziro paused his pacing when he heard the threat in Samoa's voice and said, "Is that a threat? You also forget I am an alpha as well, so you should watch how you speak to me." His voice also a threat.

The two alphas stood in a stare down for a few minutes before Samoa laughed, breaking the tension. "Oh Ziro, you are really too serious for your own good, can't even take a joke. Anyway, you heard my instructions didn't you? Doing anything contrary to that will only incur my wrath, and believe me Ziro, you don't want to do that. You may be an alpha in England, but you're on my turf now and you do as I say," Samoa said still smiling but hint of seriousness in his voice was unmistaken.

Ziro, having nothing to say to that simply nodded.

He knew Samoa was right, he had a few men here with him but nowhere near the large number of men Samoa had at his disposal. He was going to pretend to follow his orders now, but when the time came, Samoa would pay for his insolence and pride. Nodding his goodbye he walked out of the office. Samoa called Azul back in after Ziro had gone.

"The Shaman you were going to get from New Orleans to perform the ritual, has he arrived?" Samoa asked him.

"Yes, everything is ready for the ritual, we just need the girl's blood now," Azul replied.

"Good, good," Samoa said staring into space, as if deep in thought, then he looked up "Tell the driver to bring the car around, I need to go visit one of the sites," Samoa said getting up and putting on his suit jacket.

"Right away, sir."

****

Troy, Darren and Reina were in the car as they drove to Pinzu's home for the meeting, Troy had told Darren that there was no reason for him to join them, but he would not hear another word of it. He had insisted and Troy had no choice but to let him come. The three of them sat in the car.

Troy drove, with Darren beside him while Reina sat at the back of the car. They had taken safety measures while they were coming, although the vehicle that was monitoring the house had still not returned, they were still careful and Troy still had the feeling of being watched. Coldplay's hymn of the weekend blasted on the radio and Darren was singing alongside while Reina was simply looking out the window and enjoying the scenery.

Troy glanced at Darren again and smiled, how could he even be light hearted and seem so carefree after everything they had just dumped on him, he was taking all this really well, maybe a little too well and Troy was a little bit worried, lowering the volume of the radio he turned to Darren, as he drove " how are you so calm right now, after everything we've told you," Troy said gesturing to himself and Reina. Darren looked back at him, frowning a little at the radio.

"Well to be honest last night helped a lot." He smiled suggestively making Troy laugh and Reina blush hard.

"I'm being serious, Darren, I was expecting you to freak out not like extreme go crazy freak out, but I wasn't expecting this level of calmness coming from you right now," Troy told him.

Turning serious, Darren looked out the window, then back at Reina who was curiously waiting for his response. "Honestly I don't even know. I guess I'm just trying to cope with all these in the best way I can and freaking out over something I can't control isn't going to serve any purpose so there's no point in doing that. I guess trying to seem as if all these is normal is my own way of coping with it all," Darren said.

Troy nodded his understanding and reached one of his hands to clasp Darren's keeping the other on the steering wheel he whispered an "I love you."

Darren smiled at him. Reina watched the exchange with a feeling of nostalgia, she had never been loved like that, all her life she had always felt like an outsider.

These two were the only ones who had showed something relating to love. Her mind went to McCullens as she said a silent prayer for them, blessing them for saving her when they did, even though they didn't need to.

Looking away from Troy and Darren's still clasped hands, she continued to look out the window, enjoying the L.A sun on her face and the humid breeze blowing from the speed of the car, Almost one hour later, Troy drove into a very big sprawling mansion, the massive automatic gates opened as they entered and closed behind them, Darren's mouth gaped at the beautiful splendor of the home, and Reina could only gawk in awe at the house.

Luca came down again to greet them and Troy introduced him to both Reina and Darren. He cocked his brows when he saw Darren but did not say anything about it.

After the introductions, "They're waiting for you," Luca said and led them into the house, to the same room Troy had met with Pinzu the day before.

This time, there were other people inside with him, they were sitting with Pinzu in his big chair at the head of their sitting arrangement, they all watched as Reina come in,

Troy's hand instinctively went to hold her hand and she squeezed his arm as if to get strength from him.

Darren also held her hand and the three of them entered together holding hands. Pinzu eyed Darren when he saw him immediately sensing he was only human. "I don't remember asking you to bring the human," Pinzu said by way of greeting and there was a murmur from the men and women seating around him. But Darren answered even though Pinzu was addressing Troy.

"I wasn't about to let my husband walk into a trap alone in case that is what this is," Darren said showing a bravado he was not feeling inside.

Pinzu looked at him, a twinge of respect now in his gaze as he looked at Darren. "And what are you going to do to a room full of werewolves who are ten times stronger than your average weightlifter?" Pinzu asked causing some of the men to laugh.

"Anything I can to stop you from killing him or you," Darren said. "While I admire your courage and loyalty, I will not be necessary, we are only going to help you because of who she is," he said pointing at Reina.

"Let us see what she can do then," one of the men seated spoke up.

"I'm not some zoo animal here for your entertainment," Reina said. "I thought she was only going to be changing in front of just you. That was the deal Pinzu," Troy said, annoyed that Pinzu had brought all these people out here.

"My people have agreed to help you, but they want to know who we are protecting first, that's all," Pinzu replied. Troy was about to argue with that but Reina stopped him.

"It's alright, they are good people, I can sense it," she whispered to him and he relented.

Taking off her clothes gently in front of them without no ounce of shame at her nudity, Reina transformed before them into the white wolf standing tall and proud, the occupants of the room stood up the minute she began to transform, they had never seen a wolf that could change without the full moon and were all amazed by the wonder of it.

Pinzu walked closer to where she was and knelt down kissing her head. When he stood up, Reina changed back into her human form and troy quickly gave her clothes back to her to back on.

When she was decent, Pinzu started, "You have our word, white wolf. We will protect you with our life." The other men and women in the room also gave their word. Troy only felt relief at this. When they had finished settling the arrangement, Pinzu suggested Reina continued staying with them for a while, while they scouted for Nevada pack whilst they ensured that she was safe, Troy and Darren opposed that suggestion vehemently.

"No, she stays with us," Troy said, but Reina assured them that it was safer for them so they could return to work which they had already ignored because of her. Seeing the reason in what she was saying, they both reluctantly agreed.

"I will need to go back and pack my stuff for a few days," Reina said.

"Good idea, some of my people will go with you just to make sure," Pinzu added. They left the mansion to go back home and get Reina's clothes, two of Pinzu's men in another car trailing behind them. Darren had asked to be dropped off the at the hospital because of the meeting with a patient he could not ignore, hugging Reina goodbye, they dropped him off and drove back to the house together, Reina and Troy and the car still following them.

When they arrived, the car waited for them outside while Reina and Troy went into the house to the pack. "Are you sure you want to stay at Pinzu's house, you know you don't have to, he could send some of his guys to come here and keep watch when Darren and I are at work," Troy said still trying to get her not to leave.

He was afraid they had trusted Pinzu too quickly but Reina wouldn't have that, "This is the best way to keep you guys safe. The family who took me in back in England, Ziro slaughtered them right in front of me when he found me. Their death still haunts me and I won't ever forgive myself if anything were to happen to you or Darren. Ziro has a lot of men at his disposal and this man in Nevada he was about to sell me to, he has even more men, just you and Darren will never be able to take them out and I don't even you to have to, okay. This is how it's going to be for now." Reina assured him, and Troy finally agreed.

As they were climbing down the stairs, they heard some noise just outside and when Troy went to the window to check out what was happening.

He was shocked to find the two guys Pinzu had sent to protect them dead in their car, shouting for Reina to get back, but it was too late, the front door opened and two huge guys walked in followed by more men.

Troy moved with more speed when they shot the first arrow dodging it and snapping the neck of the men who threw it killing him instantly, he turned to the other guy punching him and also snapping his neck.

As he was about to turn to the other guy, he felt a sharp pain in his thighs, ignoring it, he fought the guys as they came in, taking them out as fast as he could but they were too much and he heard Reina's scream. He turned to the direction of where the scream came from, distracting himself for a few seconds when another sharp pain shot across his shoulder, this time he could not ignore it.

He felt the wolf's bane like fire as it sank into his bloodstream and fell down, blacking out. The last thing he heard was Reina's screams.

Chapter 9

It was already late by the time Darren had finished his meeting with his patient, he'd tried calling Troy but he was not picking up, so he ordered an uber. All through his meeting, he'd been so distracted even the patient could tell, he had to repeat himself a couple of times before Darren could understand what he said.

After the meeting he had wanted to go straight home to ask Troy about Reina, but he had been called by one of his supervisors who called him to go through some of his patient list and his progress so far in the hospital, like he needed the third degree today of all days.

As the uber drove him home, he thought about the events of the last few days, that night he had found Reina and Troy covered in blood, he had woken up to find the bed empty and not knowing where Troy was, he went to Reina's room to find it also empty.

He had been suspicious thinking the worst, that Troy and Reina were sleeping together but when he went downstairs and checked the other rooms, they were empty. He tried calling Troy but his phone had been on the bedside table.

He decided to wait for them in the living room until they got back from wherever they went and gave him an explanation for their absence, he hadn't even realized he had dozed off until he heard them come in naked and covered in blood.

He didn't ask any questions, he just took Reina in and treated her, and when Troy had finally told him what happened, he could not believe his ears, how had he not seen the signs, they had been together for five years for Christ sakes and he'd had no clue whatsoever.

When Reina had transformed in front of him today, he almost had a heart attack, how was that even possible that werewolves were real, and he was living with two and he did not even know. That said something about him. He was worried now about Reina, these people who wanted her dead. He only hoped this Pinzu guy kept her safe. He didn't trust him. The guy looked like a drug addict but if Reina and Troy said his word was good then he had no choice.

He could not even believe he was in a relationship with a woman now, that is if what himself and Troy had with Reina could even be considered as a relationship but he knew he cared about her, he had feelings for her, ones he'd never had towards a woman before and he knew that Troy felt the same way about her.

Their relationship was not traditional but they did not care, he was going to do everything he could to ensure that she was safe and then they would move forward from there. Deal with the problem now and then discuss their relationship later sounded like a good plan.

"Are you gonna get down or what?" the disgruntled voice of the uber driver jolted him out of his thoughts as he realized that they had arrived at his home. Paying him, he got out of the car and walked inside, the door was unlocked when he opened it.

That should have been the first sign that something was wrong, but he had seen the vehicle Pinzu had sent to guard the house, although he didn't even look inside the car, to see if the guys were in there, so he thought Reina was still was still home, but the house was eerily quiet and that was when he saw it.

Three men lying on the floor in their living room, their neck was at a funny angle showing that they were dead, he was shaking by the time he entered fully into the room and saw Troy on the floor too, rushing to hi side his hand quickly going to his neck to check his pulse.

He was relieved to feel it still beating, his breathing was weak and strained but at least he was breathing, there was a tiny injection vial on his shoulder and thighs, Darren removed it quickly surmising that it was the dreaded wolfsbane, immediately here removed it.

Troy opened his eyes and looked at him, "Reina," he muttered weakly. "They have her."

Darren lifted him to the wide sofa, and felt around him for any more signs of injury, but he found nothing.

"Who have Reina, T? Talk to me what can I do," Darren said, the urgency in his voice was present.

"Call Luca, he will know what to do." Taking out Troy's phone, Darren scrolled through looking for Luca's name and dialed his number.

He answered on the second ring.

"Hello."

"Hello Luca, it's me, Darren. Reina's gone and there are dead men in the house," Darren told him.

"Shit!" Luca said. "What about Troy, did they take him too?" Luca asked.

"No, he's here, they injected with him with, I think, it's wolfsbane but I'm not so sure, he's weak but other than that he's not too bad," Darren answered.

"Okay just hang tight, some of the guys will be over to do a sweep off and then we will talk about how we can get her back." Darren nodded as if Luca was there to see him nod. Hanging up the phone, he got Troy to their bedroom and laid him down on the bed.

"What happened?" Darren asked Troy who was beginning to heal and get stronger now that the wolfsbane was out of his body.

"We were just about the leave the house and drive her back to Pinzu's home when they came, we did not see them following us so they killed Pinzu's men outside and came in.

"I tried to fight them off but they were too many of them and then they shot me and I went down, last thing I heard were her screams," Troy said.

"Oh my God, who are these animals?" As if realizing what he said he turned to Troy. "No offence babe, but these guys are barbarians, why would they want to just use her life for their own selfish purpose?" Darren asked.

"Believe me, I agree with you, they are animals and we are going to get her back, even if it's the last thing I do!" Troy said with resolve.

Reina woke up groggy, the room was dark and she recalled the events that led her to where she was now, she cursed herself because she had once again put two people that she cared about in danger.

She felt anger now as she remembered how Troy tried to save her, he'd fought for her and what had she done, just stood there screaming like a little girl. Why did she have to be the white wolf if she couldn't even protect the people she loved, and she loved Daren and Troy, she did not know when or how it happened but what she did know was that she loved them.

She hoped Troy had survived the attack because when she escaped from this hell, she was going to show them how much they meant to her. But this time she would not just run, she would make sure to kill Ziro and his men and whoever this Nevada alpha was, she would kill him too.

Her enemies would fear her instead of kidnapping her for whatever ritual they wanted to perform on her. Ziro would pay for the hell he put her through these past few months. Looking around the room for a way out, but could not really see anything since it was so dark, she had no idea where she was since they had taken her out before they made the journey so she could not say if she was in Nevada, L.A would be too much trouble for them.

She knew they needed the full moon for the ritual and so she still had about two more weeks to think about her plan. She would bide her time and get her strength back and when the time was right she would strike. They won't know what hit 'em.

****

They had finally done it, Samoa thought to himself, the white wolf was finally in his custody, the freedom of his pack was within reach finally all they had to do was wait for the full moon. "We need to perform the ritual and we need to do it today." Ziro barged into his office, Azul coming in behind him and giving Samoa and apologetic look.

"I tried to stop him, sir," he said, but Samoa only nodded and waved him out. Ziro was breathing first as if he had just run a marathon.

"We have the girl, why don't we just perform the ritual now that we have the chance. We've already seen firsthand how unpredictable she is, we should perform the ritual and get on with our lives," Ziro said, still standing and glaring at Samoa who sat unbothered by Ziro's state.

"What you're saying is preposterous, Ziro, you know as well as I do that ritual will only work on the full moon yet you come into my office, uninvited might I add, and still suggest it. You overstep your authority, Ziro. I have had it with you thinking you can come into my club and think you can talk to me like one of your lackeys, I will not have it, so why don't you go back to wherever it is you have been staying and wait patiently until you have been summoned for the ritual, or better yet go back to England and come back in back two weeks." Samoa suggested to him.

Ziro was visibly trembling with anger but he calmed himself with great effort, he wanted to strangle the fool with his bare hands but held himself back because that would not solve anything. It would make things more difficult for himself.

Taking a deep breath and relaxing visibly, he continued, "You are right we'll wait for the full moon, I meant no disrespect," he apologized, even though it was not really a sincere one. Samoa gave him a suspicious look not buying the contrite look he used on his face, but he had nodded in acceptance.

"I want to see the girl," Ziro demanded, "To make sure your men had the right girl," he added to soften his words.

"We have the right girl, but if you want to see her, I can arrange that, we have her in a safe house, she wouldn't know where to escape to even if she somehow found a way to overpower my men guarding the place," Samoa added, with pride in his voice.

Ziro simply nodded, "Can we go now or are you too busy?"

He did not even try to hide his sarcasm.

"You do know that sarcasm is the lowest form of wit," Samoa replied him noting the sarcasm in his voice. Ziro barked out a dry laugh but ignored Samoa's comment. "I'll call my driver, we can go now," Samoa picked up the landline on his desk and dialed his driver.

The warehouse in which Reina was held was about three miles out of the city, it was deserted and isolated, an old oil factory which had been used probably in the eighties but had not been inhabited in almost twenty years, Samoa's car halted in front of the warehouse and some of the men came out and welcomed him. The surroundings of the warehouse was fortified with armed men, almost like they are protecting the World Bank.

They both walked into the warehouse with Samoa leading the way and Ziro following closely behind him. The warehouse was old and rusted. Rats scurried around the rusted engines which were covered in dust. The room where Reina was held hostage was an old office with an in suite toilet and bathroom for her to make use of.

"What do you think of our makeshift prison? I hope they are up to your standards." Samoa walked to where Reina was kept.

"Oh! I approve alright, there's no way she's getting out here and even if her two boyfriends ever dreamed of rescuing her, they couldn't know where to look. It's genius." Ziro said impressed.

Reina stood up straight from where she lay on the ground when she heard keys dangling at the door, the door opened to reveal a man she had never seen before walking in. His hair was long, almost shoulder length, he was very tall but apart from that she couldn't really see his face.

He spoke to one of the guards outside the door and almost immediately there was light in the room.

She blinked her eyes vigorously trying to adjust them to the brightness of the light. When she got used to light, she slowly looked up to see Ziro standing beside the man, they were both wearing a neatly tailored suit, making them look like sane business men but she knew better, they were just psychopaths searching for blood.

"Hello Reina. And so we meet again." Ziro said, his voice filled with glee as he taunted her trying to get a rise out of her but Reina did not give him satisfaction to see her anger, instead, she ignored him and focused on the tall man with the long hair as he was looking at her like she was the answer to all his prayers and she was.

"Who are you?" Reina asked him, totally ignoring Ziro. This annoyed Ziro and he was about to lash out at her but Samoa stopped him when he responded her question.

"I'm Samoa," he said to her as if his name was supposed to mean something to her but she only gave him a blank look.

"I'm the alpha of the Nevada pack and I need you for the things your blood can do for me and for my pack, but I think you already know that," he said as he walked towards to her.

He was not afraid she might because they had put a collar on her, which the Shaman had prepared for them. The collar was supposed to suppress her powers and tame her so she would not be able to turn. Reina glared at him, when Ziro saw this exchange he laughed out.

"Oh calm down Reina, you have nothing to worry about from him. He doesn't want you dead. All he needs is your blood. A significant amount of it. I'm the one you should be worried about because when the ritual is done. I will cut you to limb by limb until you're in shreds and whatever is left of you for all the trouble you've put me through will be given to the vultures to feed on.

Ziro told her trying his hardest to inflict fear but she could not help but laugh at the absurdity of what he was saying. She was the one who had suffered, she was the one locked up in a cage and bound like a wild animal, she was the one wearing a collar like she was a dog and Ziro still blames her for not accepting to be used for some ritual.

"We'll see about that now, won't we Ziro?" Reina said to him keeping her voice calm. Reina and Ziro both knew that even though she was the one taken hostage and chained, he was a slave to her, her powers and blood and that would never change until one of them is dead, so she stayed calm never letting him see her fears again.

No, he would be the one who feared her in the end. He would suffer for all he had done to her and everything she had been through but most of all for killing the McCullens. She was going to avenge their deaths.

Ziro noted the resolve in her voice, she looked different in the moment. The same but a little bit different, there was a new kind of determination in her voice and it left a shrill down his spine. Shaking it off, he ignored the feeling and whispered into Samoa's ear that he was leaving, he walked out of the room.

"You know you really don't have to do any of this right? There's a reason white wolves are scarce and you are about to kill the only one that's been seen in over a century," Reina said to Samoa trying to see if she could reason with him and change his mind but it was obvious that he did see her logic or he just didn't want to.

"I've spent a lot of money on you, Reina, and I intend to get my money's worth. Besides, I'm doing this for the greater good of my pack." Samoa said to her but this only made her laugh.

"Don't pretend you are doing this for a good cause Samoa, this is purely for your own selfish purposes, so don't school me about the greater good." Reina replied.

"See it how you want to see it Reina, in the end we all die, at least your death will be beneficiary and meaningful to a large number of people." Samoa shrugged as he said to her and turned to leave the room.

"You will get what's coming to you, and Ziro too. You will both get what's coming to you." Reina said to his retreating back before he slammed the door shut and clicked the lock into place. The sound of the locks made her feel like her fate had been sealed, but Reina quickly removed that thought from her head, she would not think about that, she was going to face this situation with fest and strength just the way she'd been doing all those times she was captured and she was going to trust Troy and the L.A wolves.

Although the collar around her neck prevented her from turning, she knew the wolf's bane was already leaving her blood, they needed her blood clean for the ritual, so they had stopped injecting her with the wolf's bane. She would gather her strength, she would fight and she knew that whatever happened, Ziro was not going to get the last laugh.

Samoa walked out of the warehouse to find Ziro resting on the side of his car, his legs crossed. "What do you think of the girl?" he asked. Samoa mused over that, he did not pity Ziro if that girl ever got her hands on him, but he didn't tell him that of course. "She's something that's for sure. It'd be a shame to waste it, she's got so much potential," Samoa said, "She does, I trained so I should know potential us not going to get us the power that we seek."

"You're right, but do you really have to kill her. I say if we finish with the ritual and she's still alive, just let her go. I see no reason to kill her."

"Do you really think we can let her go and she wouldn't fight back?"

"She can't fight back if she has no powers." They stared at each other for a while, then Ziro continued.

"The deal was to get her to you and you get her blood, whatever I do with her afterwards is of no concern of yours." Conceding defeat and letting it go Samoa raised his hands in surrender and walked away to his own car. They got into their various cars and drove off.

****

Troy was at Pinzu's house, he'd been coming there for over a week now. Darren had been coming with him for the first few days but he'd had to return to work. He guessed doctors were not allowed to fall sick for long.

He had taken a full leave of absence at the office, and Jane his assistant was working as a temp for another firm on his recommendation, although she would come back to him when he finally returned back to work. All he could think about right now was finding Reina, every other thing came second.

Even Darren was worried he was becoming a bit obsessed but he only ignored him. The full moon was in three days and if Reina was not found before then she would really be gone for good. He could not let that happen, he felt like he had let her down that afternoon, almost two weeks ago now.

He could still hear her screams in his dreams and it haunted him day and night. Pinzu's researcher had told them all they needed to know about the ritual and he knew it was not going to be a pleasant experience. He just hoped they found her before they had the opportunity to perform it.

He had been having recurring dreams where he saw Reina bleeding out and calling out to him and no matter how hard he tried he could never get the bleeding to stop and he could never find her. Pinzu had told him to keep trying to think of his connection to her, since was that really their only hope of ever finding her.

There was no tracking device on her and nothing to tell where they had taken her to, since no one had seen the guys who took to. All they knew was that she was probably in Nevada. A thought suddenly crossed his mind, he thought back to that night when he and Darren had been returning from the wedding.

When they had first met Reina, she had told him that she felt him near and that was why she ran towards the direction of their car that night. She had sensed that he would help her, that help was near and running towards that direction would save her. Maybe that connection became stronger whenever the both of them were closer, like say in the same state.

He knew her kidnappers would had to have taken her back to Nevada since that was where the pack was , that meant that Reina was in Nevada now and that was why he couldn't feel her or locate where she was.

He had a theory that if he went to Nevada he would be able to tell the exact location she was. He slapped his forehead in annoyance with himself, how had this not crossed her mind in the first place.

He walked to Pinzu who was still discussing their strategy for attack with some of his men in case the opportunity ever presented himself. He stopped talking when he saw Reina. "Do you know where she is?" Pinzu asked him.

"No, I don't, but I have an idea. The night Darren and I found Reina in Nevada. We'd been returning from my brother-in-law's wedding when we saw her in the middle of the road. I didn't want anything to do with her but Darren insisted we helped her, I asked Reina about that night later, about how she knew that we were going to be at that exact same place at that exact same time she came running through that road. What she had told me puzzled me, but now maybe it's not so puzzling anymore."

"Get to it, Dalton," Pinzu prompted.

"Okay, so she said she had felt that she was going to get help from whoever was coming through that road that night, and that whoever it was, was just like her. So I know this is going to be a stretch but what if Reina and I are connected because of the fact that we are from the same pack, and we also have this same exact tattoo on our shoulder, I don't know what that means but maybe if Reina can sense where I am then what if I can too. I think if we are in the same state I may be able to sense the exact location Ziro and his men have her." Troy finished.

"That's actually worth a shot. My men have been scouting the whole of Vegas and they have found nothing. This people don't want her to be found at all, but they don't know that we have you, you're our secret weapon," Pinzu said his tiny frame shaking with excitement and then turning to his driver. "Get the cars ready guys, we're going on a road trip to Vegas."

"What... what do you mean we're going to Vegas? where are we going to stay, I'm not even sure if this is going to work and besides I have to tell Darren," Troy said to him, not sure if that was a good idea.

"First I have a safe house there, two, I believe in you Troy, you can find her and three, you can call Darren on our way over," Pinzu said to them in a rush. The men were already moving around, getting ready for their trip.

They were all ready to leave in about 15 minutes and they set off for the 9 hour journey. Troy called Darren and informed him on the new development. He was against the idea for about 5 minutes, angry that he was not coming with them but Troy made him see reason, he had no choice but to agree.

*****

The sound of rats scurrying around in the dark disgusted Troy as he walked inside the darkened room, someone was muttering in a strange language that he couldn't make out what he was saying. It was probably incantations but he couldn't be sure.

He continued towards the voices as he hid behind an abandoned crane, he looked across it to see a group of men around a very high table, there was a woman on the table and she was wearing white. She was chained to the table and was struggling to get free but it seemed the chains were too strong.

The light in the room was a little bit dim so the men had not yet noticed him. Walking closer to inside the room but still hiding behind the numerous stacks of cement in a pile all around the room, he moved nearer to make certain that it was indeed Reina who was chained to the table.

Just as he was about to leave his hiding spot and reveal himself Reina's eyes met his and she shook her head, tears making their way down her cheeks. He had no plan

162

whatsoever, his plan had been to fight his way out of there, rescue Reina and get the hell out of that place.

But even Reina could see the absurdity of that plan, it was one wolf against over 15 men and he would not stand a chance fighting them alone. Now he regretted why he had not asked Pinzu's men to join him, they had offered but he was too hard-headed, and his arrogance and pride was going to cost him Reina's life.

One of the men standing around the sacrifice table followed Reina's gaze and saw Troy hiding behind one of the high stacks of cement bags.

"He's here," he said pointing to where he was still hidden, but when he looked around him the stack of cement that was hiding him just a moment ago were no longer there and the men started coming towards him.

He stood his ground and fought back but they were too many, they overpowered him and dragged him closer to the table where they had been performing the ritual.

Reina was screaming now and struggling with all her strength to get free from the chains but it only seemed to get tighter and tighter, the old man who had been muttering the strange chants produced a knife he hadn't noticed earlier and slit her throat. Troy could only stare in shock as a guttural scream left his throat and he bellowed the sounds he made was that of a werewolf howling in mourning:

"Troy! Troy! Wake up, you're dreaming wake up."

Troy jerked awake from where he had been dozing off in sleep, his neck hurting from the odd angle it was in while he had been asleep. His dream had seemed so real and he had never felt the kind of pain he'd felt when Reina was being killed right in front of him.

He glanced to his right at one of the guys who had woken him up; "Where's Pinzu?" he asked.

"He's somewhere in the house," was his reply. They had arrived in Vegas two days ago and he had been trying everything he could to locate Reina but he had found nothing. Time had not been on their side and he had not slept for the past two days because he had been so worried that sleeping was a waste of time, the full moon was tonight and they were all worried.

Pinzu had his men searching all Samoa's known places of business and hideouts but they had come up with nothing. They were at their last straw. He had just sat on the couch to think when he'd dozed off and dreamt about Reina. Standing and up and finding Pinzu coming into the room and speaking to somebody on the phone.

"I know where she is." Troy said to him. Pinzu immediately hung up the phone when he saw the seriousness on his face "But we have to go now, they're about to begin the ritual."

The men were up and moving almost immediately, the van that had brought a large number of the wolves filling up as they all piled up into the vehicle and with Troy leading them in a separate car with Pinzu, Luca and some other guy, one of Pinzu's most trusted werewolves they drove out the city.

Chapter 10

The day of the ritual was here, Samoa was having second thoughts on whether or not using the girl's life for ritual was a good idea. Like Reina said, there is a reason why only one white wolf and they come so rarely that it would be an abomination to waste the life of the only one they'd seen in hundred years.

She should be worshipped and adored and not sacrificed like some stray dog. Shaking off the thought, he realized there was nothing he could do to change anything even if he tried. He'd already paid Ziro a huge amount of money for the girl and it wasn't as if he could ask him to give him back nicely, Ziro would take him for a fool and coward.

Also the shaman was already here and he was sure news of the white wolf would have spread due to his ignorant bragging, if he did not perform the ritual now, some other pack would only come and get the girl for themselves and his park would see him as incompetent and he could be removed, he couldn't risk that. At least he was not going to kill her, that was all going to be on Ziro's. He had tried to change Ziro's mind about killing the girl but couldn't.

Ziro had this determination in him, something nobody has ever seen. He was obsessed with the girl, he could not last one more day with the girl still breathing the same air as him. But Samoa still knew that even if he doesn't partake in the killing, her blood will still be on his hands and he could not do anything about it.

His park was depending on him to perform the ritual and save them from the curse of the moon. Backing down now would only make him look weak among his peers.

Everything was in place. Azul had gone with some men to get the girl from warehouse and even though something kept telling Samoa that it could all go wrong, he ignored like he had been doing and drove to the site of the ritual.

By the time Samoa arrived, everyone was already at the site. Azul stood watch as some of the men tied her down to a table made from logs of wood joined together with nails.

She still had the collar preventing her from transforming around her neck so she struggled as hard as she could but it was useless. They would need to take the collar off for the ritual and the Shaman had warned them that when the collar was off there was a high risk that she would turn and if that happened she would be stronger than all of them joined together.

He had spelled the ropes used in tying her down to make her weak but he was not sure how long it would hold, they had to finish the ritual on time before she had the opportunity of breaking free if not they were all at risk.

He'd heard that the L.A werewolf pack were already in Vegas but they had not found them yet. He doubted they would though, nobody knew about this warehouse except his close circle, so the probability of Pinzu and his men finding them were zero to none. When he moved to join them Ziro gave him a smile that was sinister and phony at the same time but he did not read anything into, the ritual was already underway and there was nothing he could do now.

When they all stood ready the Shaman made a small incision on Reina's wrist causing her to wince in pain. He used a tiny bowl to collect the blood that dripped from the incision.

After he had done this, he walked to each of the men and made the same incision on them collecting tiny drops of their blood and mixing it all together. He then smeared the blood on their fore heads drawing the shape of an inverted triangle on their heads. When he'd covered the entire crew, he went to Reina and did the same to her. Then removing the collar on her neck he began to make the incantation for the ritual;

"Onc bina tha tieges sinc onkf"

He said this twice and then motioned for the men to repeat after him. They did and this sequence repeated itself until Reina started to shake as if she was feeling cold. Her eyes which were normally brown changed into a bright red color.

"She's changing, we have to be louder," the Shaman said to them.

The moon was not yet at its peak but Reina had already began to turn, the sound of her bones snapping as they took the shape of a werewolf rent the air and some of the men were already fidgeting as Reina got more violent on the table. The ropes that held her down were immediately broken by the time her hands and legs had been changed, the shaman moved away from the table now fear in his eyes.

Ziro called for some of his men to hold her down and Samoa did the same. They wanted to inject her with the wolfsbane to make sure she stays but the shaman told them not to do it. The men tried to hold her down and continue the chant but by this time, it was already too late. Reina had fully transformed now and all the anger she had been saving up came rushing to the surface.

She howled loudly into the night standing to her full height and facing the men. They knew immediately that she was not going to go easy on them.

*****

Troy and Pinzu's men were at the warehouse when they heard the howling. Troy knew at once that it was Reina, he guessed the ritual had started. He just hoped that they were not too late.

They all ran out of the warehouse towards the direction the howls were coming from, the moon was already at its peak and as they ran deeper into the woods they began to transform. By the time they located the place where the ritual was supposed to be carried out, it was a bloody scene they came upon.

The men were already transformed and were fighting themselves. Troy immediately looked around to find Reina, he found her almost immediately since her fur shone amongst the others, although it was now covered in blood. He immediately went to her and they immediately embraced as best as they could in their wolf form.

When Samoa's men saw Pinzu and his men they attacked, but the L.A wolfs were peaceful but vicious packs. They fought hard and Samoa lost a good number of the members of his pack that night. Ziro and a couple of his men who survived had fled the scene and Troy and Reina immediately pursued them not wanting them to escape.

They caught up with them before long. As they stood in a stare off, the two other wolfs with him attacked Reina and Troy first and they both tore them to shreds. They then face Ziro who looked like he was panicking but trying to stand tall.

"I'm going to enjoy killing you, Reina," he assured her, as they communicated by telepathy.

"It's two against one Ziro. How do you plan on doing that?" she asked as they circled one another.

"Let's do this just the two of us then. I'm sure you have wanted a go at me all these months," he taunted her referring to Troy.

Reina gestured to Troy to let her face him and when he tried to protest she gave him a look that said she needed to do this. Knowing exactly how she felt Troy stood aside and watched but was ready to jump in just in case Ziro was not all talk and he really tried to kill her.

"It's just the two of us now Ziro, none of your men doing your dirty work for you."

"I don't need them." Catching her off guard he pounced on her immediately and clawed at her eyes. Reina howled from the pain but struck him back. She felt the blood as it trickled down her eyes, but this did not deter her, they both continued to strike each other tearing and clawing the skin off of the other. When she saw an opening she immediately sunk her teeth into his neck, biting off a chink of flesh there leaving him bleeding.

"This is for John and Sarah," she said as she crushed his windpipe on the floor with her paws and he whimpered from the pain before finally going still.

Reina heaved a sigh of relief when she heard him breath his last, it felt like the ghost that had always haunted had finally been put down, and for the first time in months she could breathe again. She felt Troy walk slowly from behind until he stood right by her side and together they walked back to where the other wolves were still fighting. She had put down one bad guy but there were still more.

She searched for Samoa when they got to the place where they had just been about to use her as a blood sacrifice and found him still battling Pinzu's wolves, a large number of his pack were already dead but they kept on fighting.

"Samoa!" Reina called as she ran to their midst where Samoa stood, facing her.

"It's just you and me now. I told you it wasn't going to end well for any of you, let's get this over with," she responded in haste to spill his blood.

Samoa had an apologetic look but he had to look tough in front of his men, he knew he wouldn't leave here alive if he fought with her and he was sure Ziro was already dead as she was still here, he could see the determination and thirst in her eyes but he wanted to try.

"It's just you and me." He tried to say with the little courage and pride he had.

Reina immediately pounced on him not waiting for more sweet talk, she exerted all strength and anger on him. After what he and Ziro had put her through, he wasn't going to leave this fight alive. Lowering her head down on him, she dug her teeth into his shoulders, biting hard to draw blood. The same amount he intended to take from her for the ritual.

Without mercy, she dug her claws into his neck, ready to take to life. She kept strangling him with all strength she had left, determined to end him but something stopped her.

Samoa knew Reina was going to kill him, he knew he had lost the fight and he had no chance so he had to improvise. He whimpered in pain and made her a deal.

"Don't kill me... please don't kill me." He begged.

"That ship has sailed and wrecked Samoa, I thought you already knew that."

"You need me, Reina, don't do this. You don't have to do this." Samoa said.

"Don't flatter yourself, Samoa, what could I possibly need you for? You tried to use me against my will, so Samoa, tell me. Why should I spare you?"

"If you kill me now, what then? My park will only come after you and everyone you love. Darren and Troy will be killed right in front of you. Besides, if you kill me, other packs will just come for you to continue the ritual and they won't take pity."

"I took care of Ziro and you, I think I can take care of myself just fine Samoa."

"I can give you the protection you need Reina, no harm will come to you if you spare me."

"How do I know you are telling the truth? Why should I believe anything you say after what you did?"

"I give you my word Reina, we will make a blood oath. My pack will protect you no matter what from this day onward, I will also meet with some of my allies from other states and cities, I can convince them to also take the oath not to ever attack you and also to have your back against any other future attacks." Samoa pleaded with her.

"He has a point, Reina. We need all the allies we can get if you're going to survive. It would be ridiculous to go around killing people. Why make enemies while you can make friends?" Troy said from behind her.

She had not noticed him following her. That showed how much she had been ready to kill Samoa. But the more she thought about his idea the more attracted to it she was. She was tired of running around the world trying to escape from those who would seek to use her for whatever white wolf blood ritual they needed for their pack.

She already had Pinzu's pack firmly behind her, but she was going to need more than that in the long run. Word of the white wolf and how her blood could lift the curse of the moon had gone round all over her world and she knew that more people would be looking for her now. She needed an army of supporters if she was ever going to be able to fight back.

Releasing him and stepping away, she turned around to find them all staring at her. Both Pinzu's men and Samoa's men, Ziro's men had all been wiped out.

"Let this serve as a warning to all those who think the white wolf is going to be easy prey!" Reina addressed them all, "I am no longer going to cut my losses and run around the world, hiding from all those who would seek to destroy me, I am going to stand and fight. I am not some vessel to be used for your rituals and sacrifices. I am al were wolf. The White wolf. And I will crush anyone who dares to stand in my way. So will fight with me or against me?" Reina asked them.

There was a pause as she looked around her trying to gage their reception to her speech. Troy stepped forward and stood beside her and Pinzu did the same.

"We will fight with you," Pinzu replied.

Samoa stood up weakly and looked around at his pack. "We will fight with you," he said weakly and Reina heaved a sigh of relief.

There was a loud cheer as they all howled in jubilation. It was all over. It was finally over and she did not have to live in fear of being kidnapped or cut open for some fucked up barbaric ritual.

The moon began to lose his radiance and they all transformed back to their human form except Reina who still stood there under the moonlight. She no longer had to be afraid of her true self, afraid that someone would see her as the white wolf and kidnap her instantly for selfish reasons.

"Let's go home Reina," Troy said to her and she finally transformed back into her human form. He covered her up with a blanket and led her to where they had packed their vehicle. Samoa followed them too as they left since they had not finalized the details of their agreement. He then promised to come to L.A so they can take the oath on friendly grounds. When they all agreed they drove off back to L.A.

*****

Three weeks later

The weather was nice for camping in the woods. It was cool but not too cold and there was a relaxed feeling in the atmosphere. Reina felt it but she couldn't be sure it was in the atmosphere or just the feeling of freedom and relief that had been coursing through her veins since she signed the peace treaty with the Nevada pack. She guessed it was the latter.

Darren had been bugging her and Troy that he wanted to see both of them in their wolf form even they told him that Troy could only transform during the full moon.

He'd then suggested they go camping tonight which was a full moon, they of course could not argue with that so they had obliged him and now they were in the wood. Pinzu had promised him that his men would stay out of their way so that he would not be too overwhelmed seeing all the wolves together in one place.

After that night of the 'war', Samoa had kept his own end of the bargain. He had immediately begun to contact his allies in other cities and states. He told them about Reina and why they needed to be on her side. Although at first they had not been too eager to do that, Samoa had convinced them that Reina was worth it and she owed her his life.

The last part had done the trick. Three packs of Oregon, Arizona and Utah had already signed the peace treaty with them and counting Nevada and California they had five different packs already backing her and supporting Reina. They were not too much compared to the large number of wolf packs in the U.S but it was more than they had yesterday.

The past three weeks had been filled with a lot of feeling being revealed and scores being settled. Reina, Troy and Darren had finally talked about their unorthodox relationship. When they came back from that night in Nevada, they'd explained everything to Darren who had wanted to know every single detail of everything that had happened. Reina had tried her best to explain everything to the both of them.

Reina had also asked Troy how he had found the exact place that she was and Troy had told her He'd had a strong feeling she would be there and she had been there. They were now one hundred percent sure they had a connection between themselves since they were from the same pack.

"What do you think my parents are doing right now?" Reina asked Darren as they set up camp at the clearing they had set up for the night. Troy had gone to get some wood they would use in making a fire. Darren turned to her, wondering why she was asking something so random.

"Why'd you ask? Looks like you still think about them." He was trying to understand her mood.

"I think about them but I try not to. I mean they sold me to the highest bidder, so they obviously don't care about me. I don't know why I still bother. I hope even, that maybe one day they would come to their senses and reach out and ask for forgiveness." She paused.

"I would never forgive them of course but it'll be nice to at least see them try or make an effort." She tried to shrug it off as if it meant nothing but there pain in her voice was there. Darren would not even have noticed if he had not been paying close attention.

"I guess we never truly let go of that feeling of always needing your parents. Even when those parents are assholes, I guess kids have it wired in their DNA to always want to impress your parents, to need them to just see you. And when they don't there's always this soul crushing disappointment that we have. But it still would not prevent us from wanting or needing them," Darren said to her.

"I guess it's okay to have these feelings Reina, just don't let it get you down." Reina nodded as she thought through all he had just said.

"Hmm, look at you going all Dr. Phil on me, it's good to know that you are not just a medical doctor but also a therapist," she said lightening the mood. Darren laughed and they continued fixing the talent in silence until Reina broke the silence again;

"What about Troy's parents? He never talks about them. You on the other hand are always going on and on about your family members, I feel like I already know all of them even though I've never met anyone of them," Reina said to Darren as they worked together.

"He never talks about them, I assumed they died a long time ago. And I asked him about it when we first started seeing each other, but he was never forthcoming with the answers so I left well enough alone." Darren explained.

"And you never asked after you guys got married?" Reina asked with shock in her voice.

"I did but he never wanted to talk about it, anytime I brought it up, he would go silent for days and we would barely speak on those so just gave it a rest and stopped asking." Darren explained to her.

"Alright then." Reina wanted to know about Troy's past but now that she had heard this from Darren, she wasn't so sure about asking him about his family.

They finished fixing their tents and were arranging their stuff inside the tent when they heard Troy's approach from the forest. He came into view with an arm full of firewood and they praised him jokingly.

When they had settled down, they brought the canned foods they had brought with them for dinner and heated it over the fire Troy got going and then making a bench from a log of wood, they sat around the fire for dinner. Taking out the beers from their coolers they ate and drank in silence before Reina broke the silence.

"Troy, Darren and I were talking about how we all know our past and present but we have no info on your past except that you're from New Orleans. So what's up with that?" Reina asked him, even though she was not expecting him to give her any reply she was surprised when he started talking.

"Looks like you guys were talking about me," Troy asked them curious to know what they had been saying.

"It's not like we were talking about you babe, Reina was just talking about her parents and I was trying to cheer her up. So she brought up how we know nothing about your parents and I simply told her you don't like talking about your past," Darren told him.

Nodding his head as if in understanding he took a long gulp from the beer he had been holding and discarded the empty can.

"I don't really like talking about my past because it brings back memories I'd rather forget, memories that I don't like to remember at all. When I was sixteen my parents died in a car crash, or they told me it was a car crash, that their bodies had been burnt so badly in the crash that it was unrecognizable. They'd only identified them by their car plate which was the only thing that had not gotten entirely destroyed by the fire. We had to have a closed casket funeral so I never even saw their bodies. I was still a minor so I had to go live with my Aunt who was also a wolf. She was not married so it was just the both of us.

"For a while things were good and returning to normal, but one night in my senior year of high school. Some men broke into our house one night claiming they were looking for something my parents had stolen from the pack, some ancient relic that had been passed down since the history of the pack, but my father had stolen it and that was why they had killed him, this came as shock to me who was of the belief that my parents had died in a car crash.

"It was a full moon that night and I had just turned eighteen, when they told me they were the ones who had murdered my parents, and they also murdered my Aunt right in front of me I went into a blind rage and killed them both, and then I fled the scene of the crime. What I didn't realize was that one of the men who had come that night had been the alpha of the pack." Troy paused when they all gasped, but he continued anyway not minding their shocked looks.

"Anyway, normally a newly transformed were wolf was as strong as ten were wolfs combined that is why they have to be monitored during their first transformation. That explained why I was able to kill that Alpha and the other guy that night even though I had no idea he was the alpha.

"They sent mercenaries to scout the streets and find me, to bring me to justice for killing their alpha. They also labeled me thief and my aunt a traitor for harboring me. It was all too much, and I had no one on my side so I left New Orleans. I stayed in Texas for a while trying to lay low until the witch hunt for me had died down.

"But it only got worse and they even sent word to the wolves on the bordering states of Louisiana, Texas included that I was a fugitive and anyone who found me and brought me back would be rewarded. I had to leave Texas again and moved all the way to California, where I finally got my high school diploma. I lived in group homes for a while before I got into college, paying from student loans started working for my firm straight out of college. That's my story there, all gory details of it."

Troy said to them as he finished his story, they stared transfixed, unable to hide their sympathy for all he had been through. Darren spoke first, "I'm proud of you, T. You went through all that and were still able to pick yourself up and make something out of life. Not everybody can say that."

"I'm proud of you too, Troy. I heard stories about the fugitive but I never realized it was you. I'm sorry you had to go through all that." She said to him.

"It's alright, guys, what doesn't kill you makes you stronger right?" Troy said to them smiling and they nodded their head in understanding.

The moon was already at its peak by the time they were done talking, Troy and Reina stood up and undressed, as they transformed in front of Darren. At first he was startled by the transformation, but when he got used to them, he went close to them and they stayed like that under the moon, just together it was intimate and Reina had never felt so connected to another human being in her life.

She felt the love for these two men as it pounded in her heart. When they transformed back, she told them immediately how she felt and was glad to see that they felt exactly the same. She kissed as Darren took off his own clothes to join them naked on the blanket they had laid on the grass, they worshipped her body with kisses and when they took her, it was slow and the pleasure intense. Reina had never felt so much while having sex in all her life. They came together and it was a blissful feeling.

Reina had laid rest all her ghosts, with the help of Darren and Troy she had a future now, although their relationship was not traditional, they loved each other and that was all that mattered. They could face anything as long as they had each other.

THE END

Made in the USA
Coppell, TX
20 December 2020